THE GRANDFATHER CHRONICLES

The Secret of The Sword

Story Written by

SEAN R. BELL

Edited by
PAT RODRICKS

Illustrations by
NASTASSIA MKRTYCHAN

 FriesenPress

Suite 300 - 990 Fort St
Victoria, BC, V8V 3K2
Canada

www.friesenpress.com

Copyright © 2021 by Sean Rodricks Bell
First Edition — 2021

Illustrations by Nastassia Mkrtychan

ISBN
978-1-5255-7762-8 (Hardcover)
978-1-5255-7763-5 (Paperback)
978-1-5255-7764-2 (eBook)

1. YOUNG ADULT FICTION, FANTASY, WIZARDS & WITCHES

Distributed to the trade by The Ingram Book Company

"Engaging... [The Secret of the Sword] is fundamentally imaginative—successfully marrying Arthurian legend with modern-day Canada."
-Kirkus Reviews

"A fresh, exciting spin on Arthurian Legend, with a genre-mash up combining a mystery-thriller with fantasy, that's a winner."
-P.L. Stuart, Author of *A Drowned Kingdom*

"The Grandfather Chronicles- The Secret of the Sword is as evocative as it is riveting. Through gripping battles, stunning worldbuilding, and tapping into raw human emotion, Sean has opened the doors transporting us to an exhilarating new world."
-Keira Lane, Author of *The East Wind: A Horror & Weird Fiction Collection*

*This book is dedicated to my dear mom, who taught me:
Chase your dreams, for nothing is impossible.*

TABLE OF CONTENTS

CHAPTER
I

REUNION

On the night of May 19, 2016, the sprawling city of Toronto was, as usual, a hub of action. Traffic and people clogged the streets. Outside the Hockey Hall of Fame, crowds had gathered for the premier of Ian Dekker's *The Journey*—an eagerly awaited film that followed a young hockey player's journey to the National Hockey League.

Ian was a young man—twenty-four years of age—with an open, friendly face, and a kind smile. He had a calm presence about him as he prepared for his directorial debut. He was attractive, measuring six feet three inches with a broad chest and shoulders. His dark brown eyes contrasted with his light-brown hair. As he got on stage and started speaking from his heart about the creative ideas and stories that had helped forge his film, a silent hush fell over the now-packed theater.

After he had delivered a warm and very moving introduction to the film—in which he detailed the film's difficulties, which included contacting various hockey players, as well as funding the film himself—he walked off the stage and took a seat in the front row. Then his film played out before his eyes.

As the film's final scene faded to black, the theatre erupted into applause. An after-party followed, which included drinks, conversation about the potential positive impact of Ian's film, and his plans for future film projects.

When the festivities came to an end, Ian decided to call it a night and headed home with a wave for a taxi. Ian gazed out the window at the passing lights, reflecting on his film and the evening's events.

As the taxi dropped Ian off at his building, the late-night desk agent welcomed him with a mysterious envelope. With a puzzled look on his face after noticing the return address, Ian opened the envelope. Inside was a letter that requested him to travel to Montreal for a meeting the next day at the offices of "Foster and Smith, Attorneys at Law," at the request of his late grandfather. Ian recognized his grandfather's initials, "RR," in the bottom corner of the letter, and a tear came to his eye as he turned and headed for the elevator that would take him to his loft.

Ian entered his loft, lost in thought. He was confused, and this brought on more tears as memories of his childhood in Montreal with his grandfather surfaced after being buried for years. He had not returned to Montreal since his grandfather's death thirteen years ago. Montreal had, and always would, hold a special place in Ian's heart. Many memories of summers and Christmases still reminded him of the special relationship he had had with his grandfather for so many years. The impressions his grandfather had made upon Ian as a young child had helped to shape him into the sensitive, loyal, and hard-working man he had become.

He sat quietly overlooking the city from his loft high above the streets. It was spacious and offered an abundance of hockey, film, and collectable memorabilia. Pictures and posters of all sizes filled the eight-foot high walls, while a sixty-inch television was the centrepiece of the room. His desk also featured some very intriguing paperweights, including a trinket box with a Darwin monkey sitting on the top, examining a human skull. Another trinket box featured the Greek titan Atlas holding the world on his shoulders. There was also a small framed picture of Ian and his grandfather riding a sit-down lawnmower together.

Ian continued staring out the window with the letter from his beloved granddad in his hand. He thought of his mom, Lynn. Being an only child had created a special closeness between them, so he contemplated sharing this odd request to return to Montreal with her. However, in that moment, he decided to hold off from sharing anything until he could make sense of the decision before him.

Although the loft was only one room, it was separated into sections, with the back corner being a private area featuring a king-sized bed with night tables and lamps on either side. He headed for the right-side night table, which had a small cupboard that opened to reveal a safe. The combination lock was digital, and the code he entered was "05-20-29." "05" was for May, the month of both Ian's and his grandfather's birth; "20" referred to his birth date; and "29" was his grandfather's birth date.

The safe beeped and opened to reveal a small blue felt case. He opened the case and lifted up a 1948 London Summer Olympics Field Hockey gold medal. Ian examined the medal closely, admiring the intricate details and thinking about the amount of work and effort his grandfather must have endured to win this extraordinary piece of hockey excellence. Just as Ian was an admirer and fan of hockey, so was his grandfather years before him, and this gold medal represented a unique bond shared between grandfather and grandson. Ian put the medal around his neck and closed the safe, returning to the main area of the loft.

After emptying his pockets, taking off his tie, and carefully laying the letter down on the island in the kitchen, Ian collapsed into a brown

La-Z-Boy recliner that faced the TV. However, the television remained off, and was not the focus tonight. Instead, he pushed himself back in the chair, reclined to an almost horizontal position, and closed his eyes.

As he slowly drifted off into a light sleep, a vision appeared behind his eyelids: a small familiar sunroom illuminated with golden light. It was early morning, and the sun was just coming up. The room—which connected to a kitchen on the left, and a dining room on the right—had a warm and soothing vibe. It housed an L-shaped sofa in one corner, a reclining chair in another, and a wooden coffee table in the centre. An elderly man was sitting in the corner on the sofa dressed in a very fashionable dressing gown, sipping his coffee. He was quietly reading the *Montreal Gazette*. He had a very cool and stylish look to him, with dark brown eyes, black hair, and darker skin that seemed to glow. He wore black-rimmed glasses that helped him read the fine print of the news of the world.

Just then, a small boy wearing Teenage Mutant Ninja Turtles pajamas ran through the kitchen and into the sunroom where the distinguised gentleman was sitting. The boy was a skinny kid, no more than eight years old with brown hair and kind, warm brown eyes. The man welcomed his grandson with open arms as the young lad grinned from ear to ear.

"Ian, my boy!" the grandfather exclaimed.

"Hello, Granddad," whispered Ian in a soft voice. He then climbed up beside his grandfather and rested his head comfortably on his stomach. This was an intimate moment that had occurred almost every morning when Ian had been visiting, and in this beautiful dream, Ian was able to relive the moment as an eight-year-old child.

He and his mom, Lynn, would visit this Montreal home every summer and Christmas until his grandparents' passing. Lynn had grown up in this house, and she had also been lucky enough to call Ian's grandfather her father. Ian's mother and father had divorced when he was young, and his father had not been a part of their lives since then; so, his mom had made it a point to return to her childhood home twice a year to expose Ian to the wonderful ambiance her parents and their home had to offer. She knew the importance of family, having grown up in a close and loving one, and she wanted to pass that love on to him.

On this morning in this dream, Ian sat quietly with his granddad, looking at the paper with interest, as every so often, Granddad would share what he was reading with him. The newspaper was always delivered early, and Ian's Grandfather was always well into reading the pages when Ian joined him.

"Many stories are continued on different pages, you see," Granddad said, explaining how newspapers were organized. "The front page outlines the most important things happening, and then the story often continues on another page."

Granddad went on to explain, "In ancient and medieval times, as it is today, a person's full signature marked the ending of a newspaper article." He pointed to an article on the front page that said "continued on A2" at the end. He then flipped to that page—A2—and pointed to the end of the article, where the writer's name was typed in full: Red Fisher, who was a sports columnist for the Montreal Canadiens. "You see, my boy? The full name means that the story is finished."

Explaining further, he said, "Just an initial—rather than a full signature—often means that there is more to come, and that the story is not finished. Think of an initial as a way to continue a story on another page, or another place. It's like a bridge that connects two places." Ian's grandfather then flipped the pages of the paper back to the beginning to show Ian that indeed, the initials "RF" from an article on the newspaper's front page matched the full name on the article continued on page A2, which bore the signature of Red Fisher, thereby indicating that the story was finished.

The golden light faded, and Ian found himself back in the present day, waking up in his Toronto loft in the La-Z-Boy chair that had once belonged to his grandad. The dream Ian had just experienced reminded him of the love and joy he had experienced growing up in Montreal. He felt as if a connection that had been buried for so long was trying to resurface.

Ian smiled and said, "It's time to go back." He arranged for a flight the very next day.

Ian Dekker - The Grandson

CHAPTER
2
___

MONTREAL BIRTHDAY

To the rest of the world, today—May 20—was just another day, but to Ian, it was his twenty-fifth birthday. As the plane touched down in Montreal and taxied its way to the terminal ahead, Ian felt excited and nervous at the same time. The plane eventually came to a stop, and the seatbelt sign switched off. A voice over the intercom crackled, "*Bienvenue à Montréal*—welcome to Montreal." He waited patiently for the other passengers to exit, then fetched his laptop bag from under his seat and exited himself.

As he reached the gate area, he called his mom from his cell phone. "Hi, Mom, I'm here safely." It was early—7:47 a.m. to be exact.

"Happy birthday, my dear Ian," said a soft voice over the phone. "I wish you could have explained a little more to me about this mysterious letter you received, and why you had to leave for Montreal so quickly. I'm worried."

"Just something I need to look into, Mom. It caught me off guard, too, but anything involving Granddad deserves attention, and at this point, I don't know much more than I told you. I am curious what this is all about, and why, after all this time, my presence is needed in Montreal." Ian paused. "You know, whenever I do think of Montreal,

I think of Granddad. I had tried to bury those memories because of how much I miss him, but last night those memories started to resurface after receiving this mysterious invitation."

"I know how important he was to you, but I wish you weren't there alone," Lynn replied. "You haven't been back there in years."

"I will keep you posted, I promise."

"I love you, Ian."

"I love you, too, Mom." Ian hung up his iPhone, feeling nervous and excited at the same time. The uncertain anticipation of what this return was all about resonated within him.

As he looked around the airport, elation filled his heart, and he thought to himself, *Man, I have missed this city.* Out of the corner of his eye, he noticed a gentleman holding a sign reading, "Ian Dekker."

I guess that's for me.

As Ian approached his name, he was welcomed by the chauffeur holding it, who was dressed impeccably from head to toe.

"Good morning. It's a pleasure to meet you, Mr. Dekker. My name is Lorne, and I have been sent on behalf of the firm, Foster and Smith," said the chauffeur.

"Good morning. It's a pleasure to meet you too," said Ian with a puzzled look in his face.

"Do you have any more bags?" asked Lorne.

"Yes sir, I do, just one other small one. Thank you for picking me up," he said kindly. Ian made small talk with the chauffeur as they waited for his bag to arrive on the luggage carrousel. When the black leather duffle bag appeared, he grabbed it, but as he turned around, the chauffeur gently took the bag and said, "Follow me, sir." Ian graciously allowed him to take his bag, and they headed for the exit doors.

Neither of them noticed that since the moment Ian had set foot into the airport, returning to a place that he had not seen in years, a figure was following them. As they left the airport in a black town car, another car pulled out behind them, trying not to follow too closely and be noticed.

It was a quiet drive. Ian just looked out the window as the highway turned to reveal downtown Montreal and its beautiful skyline. Lorne told him that the firm had been looking forward to this day for a long time. "Feel free to just close your eyes and have a little nap," he said.

"I'm okay, just excited to be back and see what this is all about," Ian replied.

He was tired and could feel it, but he couldn't sleep due to mixed emotions and the adrenaline that was flowing through him.

Montreal had many wonderful attractions that made it an electric city. From the hustle and bustle on the streets, to the amazing shopping boutiques, to the delectable cuisine and dynamic atmosphere, the city had an enchanting effect on many who visited or called the city home. The Underground City of Montreal was, in itself, quite extraordinary. Many of the downtown skyscrapers and popular venues had access to the underground maze of stores and great eateries.

Lorne drove into an underground parking garage that led to the destination Ian was headed to. The building above the garage housed these offices, and it was also connected to the aforementioned Underground City.

The offices they headed for were a long way up, located on the 29th floor, and the elevator ride seemed to never end. Suddenly, the doors opened, and Lorne stepped out first. A beautifully carved "Foster and Smith" sign was on the wall ahead, and Ian was happy he had finally arrived. The office was quiet as Lorne disappeared into a back room. Ian waited patiently, taking in his surroundings and noticing all the wonderful pictures on the wall. He recognized many Montreal greats, and even a few famous actors and actresses. One picture immediately caught his eye: it was of his grandfather, smiling with his arm around one of the Montreal Canadiens' most famous icons, John Chabot. Ian was a die-hard Canadiens' fan. He had grown up cheering on the team while surrounded by Toronto Maple Leaf fans who didn't hesitate to let him know their opinions on his choice of teams—but none of that mattered now. All that mattered was that Ian was back in Montreal looking at a picture of his beloved grandfather with a Canadiens legend.

Lorne soon brought Ian into Stanley Smith's office. On the way, Ian noticed a plaque on the office door that read "Stanley Smith – Partner, Attorney at Law." Mr. Smith was a sharply dressed man with a warm and genuine smile that brought crinkles to the corners of his eyes. He had thinning hair that still boasted a youthful wave. He seemed to be working diligently at his desk, finishing up the details of the news that was to be delivered. As he saw Ian approaching, he stood up quickly, revealing his tall and lean figure.

"It's such a pleasure to meet you, Ian," said Stanley, shaking Ian's hand with a firm grasp. Ian smiled as he felt a sense of trust between them.

"It's nice to meet you too, sir," Ian replied. "I have to admit, though—I am not really sure what I am doing here."

After introductions were exchanged, Mr. Smith offered Ian his desk chair. Ian then made himself comfortable. Stanley asked Lorne to excuse them for a few minutes and closed the door behind him. He then returned to one of two client chairs that now faced Ian, sat down, opened a file on his desk, and read aloud Ian's granddad's— Reg Roberts's—wishes. "First and foremost, the house at 20 Greene Avenue, Pointe-Claire, is to be held in trust since the passing of Reg Roberts until Ian's twenty-fifth birthday."

That's today, Ian thought.

Mr. Smith continued, "The house and all its contents are, as of today, yours, Ian." He went on to explain that Smith and Foster had been holding the house until today, and they had arranged for a family to live there until Ian became the legal owner. The family previously living there was well compensated as part of the deal, and they had since moved out as per the agreement made years earlier. The firm had also been instructed to keep a close eye on the house. With that, Mr. Smith produced a brown 8.5 x 11 envelope from the file that he was reading from. As Ian accepted the envelope, he was in shock; he recognized the writing on the envelope as his grandfather's writing. The instructions written on a white label pasted in the centre of the envelope were as follows:

My dearest grandson Ian,

DO NOT OPEN UNTIL in the confines of 20 Greene Avenue when you are alone with your thoughts.

Ian left the office with more questions than answers. What was this all about? Why now, after all these years? What were the contents of this mysterious envelope? Lorne was ready and waiting outside Stanley's office to take him back to the town car and drop him off at his newly acquired house in Pointe-Claire. As the doors to the elevator closed, Ian stood quietly, holding the envelope from his grandfather close with a smile. As the elevator opened, Ian's thoughts had drifted once again with what had just transpired. Finally, a voice brought Ian back.

"Are you alright, sir? The car is just over here," said Lorne. With that, Ian shook his head and followed Lorne off the elevator into the garage and over to the car.

The suburb was about a twenty-five-minute ride from the

downtown sector. It was a friendly, peaceful neighbourhood that still looked incredibly identical to the place Ian remembered from so many years ago. Recreational parks and a private tennis club showcased the community as he reminisced about his time spent here as a child with his grandfather.

Reg Roberts had been married to Lillian Bennett. The two had been childhood sweethearts. Reg was dashing, and Lillian was beautiful. Both were pursued by admirers, but the friendship and connection that grew between them led to the kind of special bond that many people dream of.

Their beautiful home was located on a circular street also referred to as a cul-de-sac. The house came into view as Lorne drove around one of the bends. As Ian looked on at the house, he remembered this moment as a child, and felt a sense of happiness fall over him.

Lorne pulled into the driveway, parked the car, and popped the trunk. He then came around to open the door for Ian. He then proceeded to get his bag out of the trunk. Ian had kept his small laptop bag with him the entire time, and the envelope was safely inside. He got out of the car.

The house was just as he remembered it, from the stand-alone one-car garage, to the two sets of stairs that led to the house. The stairs were parallel to each other, separated by a pathway that connected them. The set of stairs to the far right of the house led to the front door, which then opened into a small entryway, with the dining room on the left and the living room on the right. Many childhood Christmases had taken place in these two rooms. The other entrance on the left-hand side of the house was the more frequently used one that led to a beautiful sunroom, where Ian had shared many early mornings with his grandfather.

Lorne led Ian up the left-hand-side steps and opened the door with a key he then handed to Ian. Lorne then proceeded to lead him into the sunroom. Ian entered slowly, embracing this moment; the sunroom looked just how it had in the dream he had experienced the night before.

Lorne spoke softly, "Anything you need, sir. Here is my card. My cell is always on, and the firm is only a call away as well." He closed the porch door behind him and left Ian to his thoughts.

Ian slowly walked around the room, taking it all in. He looked out the sunroom windows and heard his childhood memories playing in his head. He sat down in a familiar corner of the L-shaped sofa. The sofa was showing its age. It had been a centre point of this room where many discussions and friendly gatherings had taken place, each leaving its mark. So many years earlier, this was where his grandfather had sat with him morning after morning of his summer and Christmas vacations.

With a deep breath, Ian reached into his laptop bag and pulled out the envelope addressed to him. He slowly opened the envelope by ripping the edges of one side. Inside were a folded letter and a well-used leather journal. He placed the journal on the couch beside him and unfolded the letter. It read:

My dearest Ian,

If you are reading this letter, then I am no longer alive to explain things to you in person. There are things that must be brought to light that will forever change your life as you know it. It is time to share with you a secret I spent my entire life hiding from the world.

Many years ago, the High King of Britain made a great sacrifice. He was known as King Uther Pendragon, but more importantly, he was one of the pupils of the great wizard Merlin. Yes, Merlin was real, and not the fictional character you have believed him to be. He was a long-time friend and mentor of Uther. The magical wizard knew the strength, honour, and courage that his pupil possessed, and he had helped him to become High King and to unify Britain under one flag.

However, what Merlin did not take into account was Uther's sister and his other pupil, the beautiful Morgana Pendragon. She became obsessed with power and jealous of her brother, and she believed he lacked the harsher qualities needed to rule Britain. Living in the shadow of her brother's greatness fueled her jealousy, lust for power, and appetite for destruction. Her vision of the future greatly differed from that of her brother's. Her agenda was much more insidious, and Merlin knew this. He also knew that her powers were growing far too strong and evil to control. In fact, her powers now even surpassed his own, which emboldened her desire for supremacy. As she threatened to destroy the balance of power and trust that the High King had worked so hard to create, he realized what a threat his sister had become with her dark powers and malicious intent.

He knew that a wizard is forever linked to his/her apprentice, and therefore, he could not attempt to kill Morgana, for he would destroy Merlin as well. So, the wizard forged a magical sword that he named Excalibur, which would feed off the energy of its wielder. He gave this sword to Uther, knowing that the strength, virtuousness, and honour he possessed could be used to stop his sister from enslaving

Britain—and eventually the world—with darkness.

After obtaining an ancient scroll from Merlin that detailed an entrapment spell that could banish someone to a distant realm, Uther challenged his sister to a duel of wits and magic. Using the sword in an epic battle that ensued between brother and sister, Uther trapped Morgana's life force using the entrapment spell inside a crystal jewel. The jewel, which was a family heirloom passed down through generations, was bonded to the sword's hilt as part of the banishment spell. Morgana was now contained in the dimension known only as of the Realm of the Sword. This was a dark place created by the entrapment spell as a prison for Morgana.

Although the entrapment spell worked, magic must have balance, meaning for every action (the entrapment of Morgana by her brother) there must be a reaction (the spell to free Morgana was engraved on the sword, and only Uther's Pendragon Bloodline would be able to weild this sword).

The battle left the King of Britain weak and very ill due to the energy it took to open the portal to the realm within the crystal. With all of Merlin's power and Uther's last bit of strength, they buried the sword in a secret chamber deep in the castle, away from the prying eyes of the world.

As the High King of Britain lay on his deathbed, Merlin vowed to Uther that he would guard the Pendragon secret of the sword. Uther's hand fell from

Merlin's, and then the High King of Britain gasped with his last breath, "Keep the sword hidden. The power it possesses is not only too great to wield, but it contains an evil unlike any evil the world has ever seen. The sword will forever be cursed, with the darkness of Morgana bonded to it forever."

And now, since only Merlin knew the location of the sword, he devised a spell, which he engraved to his magical ring, describing where the sword was located.

As rumours of the king's death circulated around Britain, turmoil arose and tensions among the villagers grew violent. Merlin knew that evil would always flourish, so he created a second sword, also named "Excalibur," but without any magical properties, and trapped it within the Stone of Honour. The Stone of Honour was a magical stone created by Merlin that would only release the sword to Uther's heir.

This was the start of the Arthurian legend that has captivated people's imaginations for centuries. However, this myth hid the truth from the world: the sword that Arthur, heir to Uther Pendragon, pulled from the stone and used to restore the reign of the Pendragon bloodline was, in fact, a red herring. This sword was not the real Excalibur.

Merlin knew that Morgana had inspired a large number of loyal followers to her cause before her entrapment. These followers—known as Morganians—would stop at nothing to uncover the truth of her disappearance. The Merlinian Order was created by Merlin himself to protect the secret of the sword after his death—but no one was entrusted with the location of his ring, which contained many spells, including the location of the real Excalibur. The Morganians unsuccessfully led crusade after crusade for many years to find the ring and free their leader. After years of searching, the ring remained hidden from sight until a young, adventurous, eager explorer discovered its location. That explorer was me, Ian my boy.

I'm sorry to say there is a task I ask of you: to carry on what I started so many years ago as a member of the Merlinian Order. Dark powers continue their work and are closing in on the location of their trapped sorceress. Something guides and instructs the dark followers of Morgana. As my strength failed me in my later years, I was not able to carry on my mission and protect the location of the real Excalibur, as I believe its location is in danger of being discovered. I also realized a horrible truth: Morgana must be destroyed, Ian, and you must be the one to confront and destroy her.

My journal must never leave your hands, as it will help guide you on your journey to rid the world of a great evil. Pendragon blood flows in our veins, my Ian, as we are descendants of this royal bloodline, and now you must use its strength to destroy one of our own.

Remember our times together; they will help lead the

way in the darkest of times. Trust your instincts, and yours alone. No grandfather could love a grandson more than I love you. I am with you always in spirit.

Your loving granddad,

RR

CHAPTER 3

THE GIRL NEXT DOOR

After finishing the letter, Ian was in shock. He looked at the small journal that had been left to him; it lay on the couch beside him, the initials "RR" on the front cover. He flipped through the pages slowly, looking at the different pictures and descriptions. He also remembered back to the days when he would watch his grandfather complete the daily crossword, filling in the letters one by one to complete the puzzle. Ian knew the writing he remembered was identical to what he saw now, and that this was, indeed, his grandfather's journal. The pages of the journal revealed maps detailing locations all over the world. Certain locations were circled with detailed descriptions. There were also entries reflecting on events that his grandfather had witnessed or investigated, each with corresponding dates.

The journal was broken into sections: log, maps, hidden locations, and known allies and enemies of the Merlinian Order; Ian stopped at this section and noticed Morgana's name circled with lines pointing to various other names.

The final section of the journal was titled "Merlinian Elite," and this section was detailed with notes. However, while glancing over this section, he read: "The Merlinian Elite represent the most inner circle of Merlin's trusted allies and warriors."

As Ian browsed the worn pages of the information left for him, one name was mentioned time and again. Morgana's name occurred often throughout the text, and not in a good way. Much of what he had read in the letter from his grandfather was repeated in some of the more recent entries in the log section of the journal.

Intrigued and puzzled at the same time, Ian continued to browse through the journal when there was a soft knock at the sunroom door. With the journal still open in his hand and his thoughts still wandering, he got up and opened the door. There in the doorway stood a stunning figure that Ian recognized but hadn't seen or spoken to in years.

Kate Foster had been Ian's first case of puppy love, and she and her family had lived next door to Reg and Lillian for her childhood years. Ian had spent much of his childhood in Montreal with Kate, and as kids they were inseparable. She was kind and genuine with a warm nature. Kate had the girl-next-door look: brown hair with blonde highlights and big blue eyes. Her captivating smile could light up a room. She had grown into an elegant beauty, and today she was dressed in a white blouse with a denim skirt, jacket, and heeled sandals showing off her toned legs.

Ian smiled as he uttered the name. "Kate?"

"Hi, Ian. It's been a long time, and the firm notified me that you were finally back. They just wanted to make sure after all this time that a familiar face welcomed you back," said Kate in a soft voice.

Ian closed the journal and responded, "It's great to see you, *wow!*" Ian looked on in amazement at the beautiful woman his childhood friend had become.

She blushed and smiled back. "Can I come in?"

"Of course," he laughed as he stumbled to move aside and let her in.

"I remember this house, and all the great times we had in here. It still looks exactly how I remember it," she said.

She slowly walked around the sunroom—which she knew as "the porch"—taking it all in before staring out the window at her childhood home.

"How have you been, Kate? I was so sorry to hear about your dad. I wanted to come back for the funeral, but—"

"I know. After you lost your grandfather and we all lost Reg, things changed," she said.

"I'm sorry. I shut myself off from everyone and all ties to Montreal. He was such a large part of my life. Everything that Montreal was to me was because of him, and I was lost."

Kate responded, "I did try to call you a number of times. I even spoke to your mom. You just shut me out at a time when I just wanted to be there for you."

"I was young, and my life here without him just seemed empty. I left all this behind me, started fresh, and made a new life. Now it seems to be catching up to me," Ian explained.

A tear rolled down Kate's cheek. "I guess that past included me. Do you know what hurt the most? I lost my best friend, someone who I confided in. I have thought about this moment for years— what I would say to you if I ever saw you again."

"I never wanted to hurt you, Kate, and there were so many times I wanted to call you, but I just couldn't open that door again, and now, with all that's happened in the past forty-eight hours, I just need to figure things out." Ian was visibly distraught as his eyes had welled up. Everything had seemed to come rushing back all at once, and he struggled to collect his feelings and thoughts.

Kate wiped the tear from her cheek. She could sense the uncertainty and stress on Ian's shoulders. "Let me help you," she said. "Please let me in—don't shut me out again."

He turned and looked out the window, and with the position of the sun, he could see her reflection in front of him. He still didn't know what to make of the letter, the journal, coming back to Montreal after all these years, and now, seeing the first love of his life again. It all created an abundance of emotions that ran deep. The love he had for both his grandfather and Kate had been buried deep inside, and now, after all these years, it was brought back to the surface. Ian was now forced to deal with these emotions of love and loss.

He turned to her and said, "I just need some time to gather my thoughts and figure out where my place is in all this." He visibly moved away from Kate with thoughts of uncertainty.

Kate, still teary-eyed, walked towards him, gave him a hug, and quickly headed for the door. Clearly upset, she spoke softly, but with a shaky voice. "I've missed my best friend. Maybe one day I will get him back. If you decide that's possible, I'm living in NDG now, 106 Harrier Avenue." She exited, leaving him with his thoughts.

Ian remembered his grandfather's words from the letter: "Trust your instincts, and yours alone." Ian wasn't ready to bring Kate into this new mysterious world of letters, journals, maps, and legends without knowing what it entailed. He had spent many years of his life sharing his innermost feelings and thoughts with Kate, and he shook his head now knowing perhaps he could have let Kate into what was unfolding. He was also still trying to adjust to being back in Montreal after spending so many years trying to distance himself from it. Furthermore, it was clear to him that his grandfather had gone to great lengths to keep everything hidden and in safekeeping, so he was reluctant to share what he had recently learned. He slowly made his way to the corner of the sofa where his grandfather used to sit. He sat down and quietly read through the journal, more leisurely this time.

After a more thorough read-through, he closed the journal and wrapped the string binding around the small button on the cover, which held the journal shut. Ian was overwhelmed by the detailed information the journal offered him. He walked over to the kitchen area, which was connected right to the sunroom, and poured himself a glass of water using the ice machine to add some ice. "Still works, just as I remember," he muttered to himself, smiling. He realized that he was starving, and that he was very tired. On the off chance there was food in the refrigerator, he opened the door. To his delight, he saw bread, cold cuts, cheese, and pickles. "The firm really did prepare for my return," said Ian with a half-smile. He made two large sandwiches and changed his glass of water to milk, which was also in the fridge.

Even though the complicated events of the past few hours had left him dazed and confused, the familiar house and its memories helped to ground and calm him. He headed back towards the sofa with his food and milk and took off his hoodie and shoes. After devouring his dinner, he lay down on the sofa and instantly fell asleep.

He awoke refreshed several hours later, pulled his phone from his pocket, and saw a few missed text messages. He noted that two were from his mom, and the other three were from crewmembers of his most recent film; they were worried about him.

Ian quickly responded to the crewmembers, typing:

> Everything is okay, guys, just had some family stuff come up. I will be out of town for a few days. Please watch over things for me and keep me posted.

He knew there was great interest in his film due to the nature of the story, which centred around a young Canadian hockey player and his personal journey to become a professional in the National

Hockey League. There had been potential buyers and distributers in the crowd the night of the premiere. He had worked long and hard with a very dedicated crew to create the film that, at one point, had been just a dream. It wasn't like him to just run out on this potential success. In the thirteen years of being away and trying to forget everything about Montreal, there was one constant: anything involving his grandfather always received the highest priority. He then read his mom's text:

> Hi Hon, just wanted to make sure everything is okay. Been thinking of you all day and here for you when you need to talk.
>
> LUV you, MOM

Ian took some time and responded to her text.

> Hello, Mom, everything is great. Difficult to be back in Montreal after all these years, but happy to be here. Lots to fill you in on. Will call you tomorrow, heading to bed. Love always, Ian

He put his phone down on the table and noticed the reflection of the RR on his glass from the letter; it was the same "RR" as on the journal. He referred back to the letter, again noticing the bolded "RR" at the end, and then remembered back to something his Grandfather had said to him: "Signatures are permission or ownership for something." He smiled and remembered one other thing he had said: "Initials can mean there is more to come." He then realized that the initials on the letter and journal were a code; his grandfather was talking to him even now, telling him that a story was continuing.

CHAPTER
4

SECRETS OF THE PAST

Ian rushed to the basement, as he remembered that this had been his grandfather's part of the house where he kept many things that had a personal meaning to him. Ian had spent time down here with his grandfather on many occasions; whether it was watching the Montreal Canadiens and being treated to the wisdom of a life-long fan, or just being able to spend those precious moments with someone so special, these basement walls echoed many memories of Ian's past.

The downstairs of 20 Greene Avenue was a cool, dimly lit place that was isolated from the noises of the house and the outside world, it seemed. As he went down the stairs, the room opened up to reveal a spacious area with a well-stocked bar and bar stools. It was a cozy environment that included a large antique television, two soft sofas positioned at ninety degrees to each other, and a comfortable chair with a footstool; this was his granny's chair, and he noticed the empty space where his granddad's La-Z-Boy recliner used to be. Just off the sitting area was a bedroom with sliding doors for privacy. The bedroom connected to a bathroom with a shower that was tucked in behind the bar area. Ian could tell the basement had been kept intact for him, just as the rest of the house had been. The atmosphere down here was just as Ian remembered: calm and soothing.

This is where his grandfather had his own private domain. And everything was, once again, just as he remembered it. The walls had a collage of pictures showcasing great moments and wonderful memories of times now passed. He looked upon a picture of his grandfather and grandmother celebrating with friends in little pointy hats the start of a New Year. As his eyes followed the pictures on the walls, he also noticed his mom and grandfather sharing a picture together; Ian smiled at the picture's warm embrace. He always enjoyed spending hours down here.

He paced the room slowly, smiling as if he was reliving each picture and memory that he could recall. His eyes scanned every picture, and every corner of every picture, looking patiently for what he now knew had been left for him to find. He heard a voice in his head from a memory a long time ago: "Patience, Ian. Remember the P word, my boy." His grandfather's voice was not one he would ever forget. Having patience was something that Ian's grandfather had tried to engrain in him, and all these years later, it was still something Ian struggled with.

Out of the corner of his eye, he noticed an 8.5 x 11 picture hanging on the wall. This specific picture was of his grandfather, grandmother, his Aunt Tessa, his mom Lynn, and himself all in a line on the front yard of 20 Greene Avenue. This picture was at least twenty years old now, and everyone in the picture had his or her best smile on. Ian's eyes welled up as a tear now rolled down his right cheek. As he continued scanning the picture, he noticed another small "RR" in the bottom right-hand corner. He carefully took the picture off the wall and felt around the corners and frame, but he couldn't find anything out of the ordinary. As he continued feeling around the back of the frame, he felt a lump. It was a folded piece of paper, taped to the frame, right behind the "RR."

He returned upstairs with the picture, looking at it more closely now. He put the picture face down on the kitchen table and carefully removed the piece of paper. He unfolded it to find a picture of a child with an elderly man; it was Ian and his grandfather, embracing with the joy of family at Christmas. That was a moment in his life that he would never forget. Although he could not remember how old he exactly was in this picture, he remembered that that Christmas had been a significant one, because of the special gift he had received from his grandfather.

Just as he looked up to bring his thoughts back to the present, a shadowy figure sitting on the sofa in his grandfather's spot greeted him. "Hello, Ian," she said. "It's nice to finally meet you. I have heard a lot about you."

The shadowy figure came into the kitchen, and Ian's heartbeat raced as the faint light revealed a woman dressed in black robes. Ian, not sure if his eyes were playing tricks on him, jumped back at the intrusion of this figure. "I think you have the wrong house," exclaimed Ian, his voice loud but a little shaky.

"No, no, I have the right house. My apologies for alarming you, Ian," said the mysterious figure as she approached Ian slowly. "I've never been good at introductions. I'm Isabella, and I've been sent by the Order of Merlin to protect you." She was a slender, attractive, older woman with a determined look in her eye. Her hair was dark brown and tied back. Her eyes were kind, but mysterious.

Ian collected himself, now scratching his head. "Wait, this is crazy—I was just reading my grandfather's notes on this Order of Merlin. How did you know I would be here, or who I am even?" he asked. Ian made sure that with every step Isabella took toward him, he took a step back, keeping his distance the best he could. There was a pause before Ian asked, "What do you want from me?"

"We have been waiting for this day for a very long time, Ian," Isabella replied. "Your grandfather was more than just a member of the Order. He was an *Elite*—a high-ranking Merlinian responsible for the protection of the sword, Excalibur."

Puzzled, Ian folded up the small picture and secretly put it in the left pocket of his jeans while responding, "This is crazy. It's all happening so fast. Why now?"

"I know you have questions, and I have answers for you, but right now, we need to leave." He could tell she was on edge as she frantically walked from the kitchen back into the sunroom. Her eyes scanned the dark street through the windows as if she was looking for something or someone. "Since your arrival earlier today, you have been watched," she said.

"Watched? By whom? I don't even know what's going on anymore," he said.

"They call themselves Morganians. They are loyal followers of the sorceress, Morgana. They want the sword and will stop at nothing to get it. I have also been following you." She smiled to try and ease the tension of the moment, but her eyes continued to show the seriousness of the situation at hand. "Please, just come with me. I promise I will explain everything to you, but right now we are not safe," she exclaimed as she grabbed his hand. "Your grandfather built a secret passage out of the house from the basement for circumstances such as this. Let's go—*now*."

Ian, reluctant to trust this woman, thought to himself, *She knows details of who I am and who my grandfather was.* He needed answers to so many questions, and right now, this Merlinian woman was his best bet. So, he decided to go along with her. Ian quickly grabbed his jacket and put it on. He folded the letter from his Grandfather that was sitting on the table in the sunroom. He then tucked it into his right jacket pocket, then, grabbed his grandfather's journal and his cell phone along with his laptop bag, which he put over his shoulder.

They raced down to the basement. Isabella led the way to the bedroom and opened the closet door. The metal rod that was used to hang clothes on was lying on the floor. "I removed this when I came into the house a few hours ago," she explained. "I kept my distance, Ian, watching the property and surrounding areas for any unusual activity. When I caught a glimpse of a few suspicious shadows, I knew I had to get you out." She then removed a small key from her belt and inserted it into a small keyhole on the bottom of the closet's light switch plate; the light switches were black, as well as the cover plate, so it would be very easy not to see the little hole. She clearly knew her way around.

"How do you even know to do that?" Ian whispered.

"Your grandfather showed me a lot in the time we spent together preparing me for this day." As she turned the key, a hidden door slid open in the back wall of the closet. She opened the door wider and stepped through, turning on a small light at the top of a staircase. "Watch your step." Ian followed her down. When he got to the bottom, there was a string of small illuminated lights leading the way through an underground passage. "Let's go," urged Isabella.

They continued along the lighted passageway until they could go no farther, as they came to a wall that seemed, at first glance, to block their way. Again, Isabella took out the small key and inserted it into a keyhole that was located near the ground and out of sight; again, this keyhole could be easily missed if the keyholder did not know where to look. Another hidden door opened from this wall with the turn of a key, and this secret chamber now gave way to the outside. They exited, now finding themselves at a small, local train station not far from Greene Avenue that Ian remembered visiting as a young child. She closed the door, which locked behind her, and he followed her to a black Lexus SUV in the train station's parking lot.

She opened the front passenger door for him, and then got into the driver's seat. She started the car, the engine purring to life, and they sped away in an instant.

Isabella calmly but firmly asked that, for the safety of the Merlinian Order, Ian blindfold himself for the duration of the ride. Trying to feel as relaxed as he possibly could, he agreed, taking the black blindfold that she offered him. Taking a deep breath, he tied the blindfold around his head. Now peering into darkness, he heard her voice saying, "Just a ten-minute ride, and we'll be there." He put his head back against the headrest and continued to listen while she drove.

She headed onto the highway into Montreal. She knew that he had questions, and as promised, she started revealing information. She confirmed that the Roberts and Pendragon bloodlines were one and the same, and just as Reg's letter to Ian had outlined, he was requested to carry on his grandfather's Merlinian duties. Because of the special relationship they had enjoyed, Reg had entrusted his life's work to his grandson.

Isabella said she knew of a safe place where they could regroup and plan their next move. A Merlinian safe house was their destination hidden in the downtown area of Montreal. "Time is running out, Ian," she said. "For the first time in thousands of years, the Morganians are a real threat to the survival of humanity."

Ian remained calm and quiet, but in a determined voice he said, "I'll do whatever it takes to protect my loved ones." He sensed through his blindfold that she was smiling. For the remainder of the car ride, there was silence but plenty of thought as he continued to process this world he never knew about but now was a part of.

CHAPTER 5

THE MERLINIAN ORDER

The car ride was anything but relaxing as Ian sat waiting anxiously for the mysterious destination to be revealed to him. Thoughts rushed through his head about his grandfather, the letter, the journal, and this secret of a hidden sword passed down to him. Despite everything that had been revealed to him thus far, he remained calm.

As the Lexus jolted to a stop, he heard a car door slam and then heard his passenger door being opened. Isabella gently grabbed his hand and helped him out of the car. With the blindfold still securely wrapped around his head, she guided him to their destination on foot. With his other senses now on heightened alert, Ian's nose picked up a musty smell that reminded him of candles and incense. He felt himself descending a narrow stairwell that wrapped its way downward. This mysterious walk seemed to go on forever, with Isabella leading Ian carefully.

Finally, she untied the blindfold, and he had his sight restored. "Welcome," Isabella said. "You are standing in one of the oldest Merlinian temples in the world." Ian looked around him. They were in a massive, three-level structure that was circular in shape and made of stone. They had entered onto the third level, and he gazed down in awe at his surroundings. The lowest, first level had a statue of a wizard surrounded by several huge, ancient altars, which were also in a circular formation. The second level was a few steps up and consisted of a balcony with a beautiful carved railing that overlooked the lower level. The third and final level, which they now stood on, was a few steps higher again, and it was a gallery that overlooked the bottom two levels. The walls were engraved with images and descriptions of times passed.

Ian was drawn to a magnificent image of a battle that seemed to be the main focus of this entire wall where you entered the temple. Other images branched off from it. He remembered reading about this particular battle in the letter from his grandfather. He recognized the sorceress Morgana locked in a magical battle with her brother Uther. As he walked around the third level, he noticed small stone tables with stone blocks to sit on. Shelves carved into the stone walls housed scrolls and ancient relics that had become victims to the elements of time. He also noticed a circular indentation in the ground that stretched around the entire level.

Isabella explained, "This is the uppermost circle. These great temples were both schools and libraries for the Order. The Order itself was founded to protect the location of the real Excalibur, but other teachings were passed down through the generations to protect the world from the dark forces wanting to surface."

Ian listened attentively as he stepped down the stairs to the second level. Again, this level featured another circle engraved in the ground. He asked, "Another circle?"

She explained further, "The three levels of this temple, which is circular in shape, represent the three Merlinian circles. The uppermost level is where students would study and learn Merlinian history and art. Studying on the second level meant that your knowledge and understanding of Merlinian teachings was growing to a certain potential. To move from circle to circle demonstrated an understanding of teachings and trust in what Merlin created."

"What *is* a Merlinian?" he asked.

"A Merlinian is, above all else, a protector of this Earth Realm from the forces of darkness. There are many realms that are all connected, and many ancient evils prey on innocent lives. Our job as Merlinians is to stand against these dark forces," she said.

"Like Morgana?" he said.

She took a deep breath and responded, "Morgana is the greatest evil this earth has ever known. Once a pupil of Merlin, she craved power and control and never respected wizardry—the practice of harnessing the energies that surround us to create magic. She abused the power she possessed for personal gain, hurting others for her benefit. In doing so, she devoted herself to evil. Legends say that before her brother Uther trapped her, she was even more powerful than Merlin."

Ian replied, "Yes, I remember reading some of the details in the letter from my grandfather. Even the journal he left me has extensive notes on her and her followers."

Isabella had worked her way down and was now standing on the second level of the temple. Then she slowly stepped down to the first level and walked around the massive altars encircling the statue of Merlin, all connected again by a circular indentation in the ground. "Elites are powerful Merlinians who are well trained in the art of wizardry, and they possess unique qualities that allow them to play intricate roles in the balance between good and evil," she explained. "They are represented by this third circle. As you now know, your grandfather was a Merlinian Elite."

She explained that Reg had been one of the highest-ranking Merlinian Elites and had sworn an oath to protect the location of the Merlin Ring; this was the great wizard's ring that his grandfather had mentioned in the letter, and it was the key to the location of the real Excalibur. Ian remembered that he had read in his Grandfather's journal that no one except for Merlin had known the location of the ring until his grandfather had found it.

One of the few remaining Merlinion Temples - located deep below the streets of Montreal.

The Merlin statue on the first level or bottommost level had one final indented circle on the ground around it; this was the closest circle to the great statue of Merlin.

"There are only a select few who have ever achieved this inner-most, or fourth circle, of Merlin," Isabella continued.

Ian nodded and spoke with confidence, "Merlin and Morgana."

She nodded. "To possess that kind of power is unthinkable. There have been whispers over the years that Merlin would appear to help guide only the most dedicated of his order. I myself have never seen the great wizard, but it was always taught that his life force lives on in a realm far beyond our own." She paused for a moment and then carried on. "The greatest fear the Order has is the release of Morgana's life force back into the Earth Realm. Her followers grow in numbers every day, and rumours are now spreading that a powerful witch, Abigail Williams, guides their every move."

"There's only one answer, Isabella," Ian said. "We have to find the sword and destroy it. As long as it's out there, it can be found."

She reacted by saying, "If your grandfather found the Merlin Ring, Ian, I believe he would entrust its care to you. It can lead the way to the location of the real Excalibur," she said.

Ian thought about the first clue he had figured out back on Greene Avenue; the picture still remained hidden in his jeans pocket. He carefully took it out and approached her. He placed the picture on the altar and opened it. "This is my granddad and I many years ago. He is trying to tell me something with this picture, as he left clues for me to find it." He still did not fully trust Isabella, but he had so many questions he wanted answers to, and she seemed to be his best resource at the moment.

Ian focused on the picture; it was speaking to him, trying to tell him something, and suddenly his eyes widened. "I need to get to my friend, Kate," he said. "We need to find the ring, and Kate has something that will help us. I'll explain on the way. Trust me."

Isabella nodded and, as she moved towards him, smiled and said, "You are very much like your grandfather." She pulled out the blindfold and said, "No need for this anymore." She tucked the blindfold back into her robes. Ian then followed her up the stairs, exiting the temple.

CHAPTER 6

THE MORGANIAN MONKS

Notre-Dame Basilica is the most beautiful church in Montreal. Its architecture and unique style attract people from all over the world who marvel at its beauty. The niches, running parallel to the nave along the sides of the building, are coloured deep blue and decorated with golden stars. The central part of the sanctuary is decorated in azure, red, purple, and silver. It is filled with hundreds of intricate wooden carvings on the walls and many religious statues. The area surrounding the altar, as well as much of the altar itself, is a blaze of gold. Unusual for a church, the stained-glass windows do not depict biblical scenes, but rather scenes from the religious history of Montreal.

As Ian and Isabella ascended the stairs, Isabella explained that the Merlinian temple in Montreal was located directly beneath this extraordinary church. Unknown to millions of tourists who visit every year, Notre-Dame Basilica houses a secret passage to the great temple below. Behind the amazing, eye-catching altar—which is the centrepiece of the Basilica—is a hidden door that is part of the altar itself, and it can only be found by those who know it exists.

This door opened slowly from the inside, and Ian and Isabella emerged. As they entered the church, which was empty this time of night, they headed down an aisle that led to the back of the church, where they could exit onto the street. At night, as it was now, the city looked beautiful, with a multitude of lights bringing it to life.

As Ian approached the parked Lexus, he turned and said, "I'll drive, Isabella. I know the way to Kate's place." She handed him the keys, they got in, and the car sped off as he turned on the engine. It was a Friday night, and the traffic on the streets and the crowds of people made the downtown core quite congested. She listened as he explained.

"My granddad always liked to test me, and even now, he's communicating to me, through clues he has left from times we spent together." Ian pulled out the picture he had kept in his pocket with his right hand and handed it to Isabella, keeping his left hand on the wheel. "See the kid wearing a Montreal Canadiens jersey? That's me. I loved the Montreal Canadiens as a child, and my dear granddad was the reason for that. He explained the game of hockey to me, as well as the rich history of the Canadiens. I'm telling you, I collected so much Montreal Canadiens memorabilia. A lot of it was lost over the years through various moves, but a few items were kept and stored away." He hesitated for a second, and then continued, "After the death of my granddad, I was lost, as part of me died with him, and I buried that part of me. I needed to leave everything that reminded me of him in the past, including returning to Montreal. I entrusted one very special item from my childhood to my best friend, Kate: my very first Montreal Canadiens jersey, given to me by my granddad."

Isabella smiled softly, but it was quickly erased as her eyes glanced to the passenger side-view mirror.

"We have a tail, Ian," she said, quickly handing the photo back to him.

"That didn't take long," he responded as he looked into his mirror.

Isabella continued, "The black sedan with the tinted windows two cars back. It's been with us for a few miles now. It could be our enemies." She explained, "Morganian Monks—magicians who are loyal followers of Morgana. They use their energy to create dark magic. One of their greatest abilities is that they can create duplicates of themselves called Phantoms. Your bloodline can see them, but most people can't; they can see the destruction left in the Phantoms' wake, but they never see the Phantoms themselves. Just as Merlin left behind scrolls and the teachings of his ways, so did Morgana. You must understand that the Merlinian Order has been battling these Morganians for a very long time, and as their numbers have grown, ours have diminished. There are only a handful of Merlinian temples left now due to the conflict that has raged for hundreds of years. The Order itself is all but extinct."

He responded, "I have to get to Kate and the jersey. The picture is the clue, and the jersey is the next step."

She nodded and said, "At the next light, take the metro and get to her. I will try and hold off the Morganians tailing us by diverting their attention, but you won't have much time."

As they approached the traffic light, Ian noticed Isabella was wearing a beautiful ring made of gold with the letter "M" on it. The car halted at the light, and he shifted into park. At that moment, Isabella hopped out, and using her ring, sent off a ray of white light in the direction of the tailing sedan, creating a blinding effect. "Don't look into the light," she said, "and go—*now!*" He bolted from the car, taking his bag and leaving the dazzling light behind him.

As Ian darted through the streets of Montreal, he noticed dark hooded figures that he now knew were Phantoms: projections from various Morganians, popping up in the crowds of people he passed. He weaved in and out of the busy downtown crowds and headed to the Bonaventure Hotel, which had an entrance to the Underground City, where he could catch the metro.

He crouched down and hid behind a small group of people for a moment near the Bonaventure metro platform. He remembered something he had seen in his grandfather's journal, in the section called "Adversaries." He pulled out the journal from his bag, flipped through the pages, and stopped on a page that had notes on dark forces in combat. He read the notes quickly:

> Morganian Monks can create shadows of themselves called Phantoms. These Phantoms are dangerous because of their dark powers and their ability to attack in numbers. To stop them, you must defeat the Source Magician who has created them in his image. He must always be in close proximity to them. Source Magicians are Morganian Monks, and they can be identified by the red ring with an "M" on it that they wear. It symbolizes their loyalty to Morgana. They are in a weakened state when conjuring Phantoms of themselves because of the energy it takes to conjure and control them.

He continued reading that Phantoms represent dark magic, and since the world depends on balance, good and pure magic can conquer the Source Magicians, especially in their weakened state.

The metro car approached and came to a complete stop before the doors sprang open. Ian glanced around tentativelly, closed the journal, and tucked it into his bag. He quickly boarded the metro and grabbed a pole to help stabilize his balance as the doors shut. He heard the unique chime that signalled the departure of the metro car from the station. He continued to move quickly through the car as he saw two Phantoms pop up behind him. The metro car glided smoothly along the tracks as he continued to move swiftly, grabbing poles as he went. He stopped in an empty car toward the end of the train. As he paused for a moment, he noticed that the pendant he wore around his neck had begun to glow white. The pendant was small and circular, made of gold with a small emblem of a saint in the centre. The small words engraved around the circle identified this saint as Saint Christopher: the protector of children. Ian wore this pendant all the time.

As he watched it glow, he felt a sense of warmth and love fall over him, and he smiled. The pendant had been a gift from his mom, and he gently grabbed it in his hand as he recalled her words: "Saint Christopher will always protect you."

Just then, a dark Phantom appeared right beside him and grabbed his arm in an iron grip. A chill ran through Ian, as he could feel himself caught in a mental trance. He thought of his mother and how special this pendant was to him; it was a precious gift that he treasured. Suddenly, he knocked the Phantom away with such force that it threw Ian through the air as well, landing him at the back of the metro car.

Getting to his feet, he realized he had fully recovered from the trance that was brought on by the Phantom's touch. As the metro car came to a stop, Ian heard the metro stop on the intercom, "Vendome," and the doors opened. He exited through the doors and continued on foot towards Kate's house.

CHAPTER
7
___

INNER STRENGTH

Kate lived in NDG (Notre Dame de Grace): a suburb of Montreal. The Vendome metro stop was a few minutes' walk from her place. He knew his way around Montreal quite well. When he used to visit his grandparents, they would frequently go into downtown Montreal by car or metro so, he had become very familiar with the city, its surroundings, and its landmarks. Just to be sure, Ian took out his cell phone, and using his GPS, confirmed Kate's address.

His heart was pounding as he approached the door to Kate's brownstone. It was just after 11:00 p.m., according to Ian's phone. He knew he needed to include her in the events that were unfolding as soon as possible. He walked up the steps to the door and rang the bell. He heard light footsteps, and then the door opened to reveal Kate in her dressing gown, shocked to see Ian standing there and out of breath.

"Hi, Kate," Ian said. "I'm sorry for the intrusion this late, and I know you are upset with me, but I need to talk to you."

She had a worried look on her face, as he was in a bit of a frantic state. "Are you alright? What's going on, Ian?" she asked as she grabbed his hand, pulling him inside and closing the door.

Her place was warm and inviting, dimly lit with a few candles burning and a lovely feminine incense scent. The hallway went straight back from the front door to the back door, and arched doorways on both sides of the hall gave way to large living areas. The left side had two openings: the first one went into the living room; the second to a kitchen that was connected to the dining room and living room. On the right side of the hallway was the master bedroom with an en suite bathroom. There was also a powder room and a guest bedroom with an attached bathroom on the right side of the hallway.

Ian paced the hallway and began explaining this new life of his that was unfolding. Kate listened attentively as he explained the letter from his granddad, the journal, the Morganians, the Merlinians, and the house at 20 Greene Avenue being left to him. These were only bits and pieces of the greater story, but it was enough information for her to grasp what was happening. She trusted Ian, so her reaction was calm, but at the same time, she was concerned. She had some information to share, as well.

Her father had been Reg's attorney and friend and had been in charge of his estate. Ian was surprised to hear that Kate's late father had given her a letter with instructions that pertained to him. She handed him her cell phone, which she had used to take and store a picture of this letter. It outlined a number of things specific to her, but also things related to Ian: that certain items be kept safe for him; that the ownership of 20 Greene Avenue would go to him; and that the firm would request that he return to Montreal on his twenty-fifth birthday. These were his grandfather's wishes, so Kate had known he would be back. Ian skimmed this letter on Kate's phone.

Kate had also been instructed to tell him about the items the firm had in safekeeping for him once he had read the letter from his grandfather. Even Kate didn't know what these special items were, just that they were meant for Ian. She explained that she had called the firm earlier in the day, and they had notified her that he was in town. She went on to say that as much as she had wanted to tell him what she already knew when she had first seen him, she couldn't until he had read the letter, even if it upset her that he initially wanted to keep his distance.

Thus, as it turned out, it didn't take Ian long at all to bring Kate into this new world and make her part of his family mystery.

Ian took out the folded picture he had found back at 20 Greene Street with the help of his grandfather's clues. He opened the picture to show her, and she smiled with moist eyes. He pointed to the Canadiens jersey he was wearing in the picture. "Do you remember this jersey, Kate?" he asked.

She nodded, motioning for Ian to follow her as she headed for her bedroom. He returned the photo to his pocket, then followed and watched as she opened her dresser drawer and carefully unwrapped the jersey from a protective white cloth; he was touched by how she had looked after it over the years. He walked over, hesitating at first, and then put his arm around her as she held the jersey. She leaned her head on his shoulder as she wrapped the jersey up again and gave it to him. He was incredibly moved, holding the jersey from his grandfather. As she kissed him softly on the cheek, she noticed the pendant around his neck.

"Ian, your pendant is glowing!"

"Is it? The same thing happened when I was on the metro, but I don't know how or why it does that." Then Ian connected the glowing pendant to his encounter with the evil Morganian Phantoms on the metro. "But I think we have to leave now. It's not safe."

"Okay, I'll get dressed," Kate said, believing him.

While she changed, Ian headed for the kitchen. He could feel something was off. Just then, he heard a creak in the floor. He exited the kitchen into the hallway, just as an M-shaped dagger flew in his direction. The weapon was crafted as an "M" with a sharp dagger extending from the middle of the M downward. He jumped back to avoid it just in time. Out of the corner of his eye, he saw a hooded figure just inside the front door—and then suddenly, the hooded figure became two. Horrified by what was happening, Ian quickly went back into the bedroom.

"We need to go now, Kate," he said.

Kate had now ditched her nightwear and was wearing a T-shirt with jean shorts and sandals. She grabbed her keys off the dresser as he took off his jacket and put it around her. Ian kept his bag, putting the strap around his neck. He took out the journal from his jacket, put it in his bag, and then gave her the jersey to conceal inside the jacket. He shielded her, and the two went running across the hall to the kitchen and ducked behind the island.

"Where did that dagger come from?" Kate asked, now looking at the dagger shaped like an "M" lodged into the wall by the entrance to the kitchen.

"Morganian Monks," Ian replied hastily. "they use dark magic energy to create shadows of themselves called Phantoms. We have to find the Source Monk. They're already inside, and they attacked me. We have to get out."

Confused, she asked, "I don't see anyone."

He explained, "Apparently, not everyone can see them, but trust me, they are here, and they are after us."

The Saint Christopher pendant continued to glow as they snuck onto the back deck through the door from the kitchen. Kate insisted the two make a run for it to her car in the garage below the house. "We can take the stairs down from here," said Kate.

"I have to stand up to them," Ian said. "They want me, Kate. Get to the car. I'll meet you around front."

She nodded, then headed down the stairs leading from the deck to the garage.

Ian closed his eyes and whispered, "Come on, Granddad, please talk to me."

He felt a jolt, and suddenly for a brief moment, he was seeing through the eyes of the Source Monk. He looked down and noticed the black robes he was wearing. He was crouched down, hiding next to the stairs leading up to the front door of Kate's brownstone. Being connected to something evil, he felt a sense of coldness inside, even if it was only temporary.

He remembered the events on the metro, and how he was able to use some sort of inner strength or power to repel the monk trying to capture him. He held the pendant close and thought of his mom. Suddenly a beam of light shot out from the pendant, stopping at the wall in front of him. The beam seemed to be a source of white light that Ian could control for his protection, so he opened the door to the kitchen and stood in the doorway. The beam ricocheted off the walls in multiple directions, hitting all five Phantoms in the apartment. Ian noticed that they were now frozen, so he darted for the front door.

As he headed down the steps to where the Source Monk was hiding, his pendant began floating in front of his neck with tremendous energy. Then, just as he had done on the metro, he closed his eyes and thought of a loving memory. He thought of his mom again, and of the day he had been given the pendant for his nineteenth birthday; it was to protect him as he journeyed out into the world. He closed his hand around it. Then he opened his hand slowly and directed all the energy at the motionless Source Monk. There was a flash of light, and the Phantoms and the Source Monk vanished into the white light.

Ian collapsed to the ground. Kate had pulled up to find him in a weakened state; she helped him into the car, and the tires squealed as the VW Bug drove away. He reached over and held her hand on top of the gearshift. "Thank you," he whispered. He insisted that they needed to get off the grid and make sense of all that was happening.

"I know just the place—sleep now," Kate replied.

Ian's eyes closed at last. He felt he was exactly where he needed to be.

CHAPTER
8

PRECIOUS GIFT

Soft, golden light surrounded 20 Greene Avenue once again as Ian dreamed another powerful childhood memory. It was Christmas time, and no one loved Christmas more than Ian's grandfather had. Christmases were a very special time for young Ian because he was exposed to such wonderful family traditions. The tradition that was his favourite was decorating the Christmas tree. Every year, he would arrive in Montreal for Christmas to the house decorated; the stockings were hung over the fireplace, the garlands were draped over the mantle and mirror over the fireplace, and Christmas cards were strung and hanging on the walls. Decorations were scattered around the rooms on various tables. Delicious aromas wafted throughout the house due to his grandmother's exceptional cooking.

At the centre of it all was a big, real, live tree (of course!), undecorated except for the lights; the decorating of it was the special task Granddad would leave for his grandson. It stood proudly in the living room in front of the big window, and usually the day after Ian arrived, he would begin decorating. His granddad would have all the boxes with the special ornaments and keepsakes ready for him to unpack and display on the tree. Even the task of making sure the tree had water fell to Ian, and his granddad always gently reminded him of this every morning. These times in Ian's life were special because they further cemented the special bond between grandfather and grandson. The outside world didn't matter; it was like being trapped in a snow globe and never wanting to leave because everything was, simply put, perfect.

The dream Ian was having now was of Christmas morning, 1991. The house was quiet. Ian was ten years old, and the first thing he did that morning was water the tree. Granddad was already awake upstairs. Even though they were both early risers, there was an understanding that the eagerness to open gifts had to wait until 8:00 a.m. It was currently around 6:30 a.m., and this meant that Ian had to wait before waking up his granny, his mother, and his Aunt Tessa. He would watch the clock impatiently, but he loved every moment he waited with his granddad.

This particular Christmas morning was a memorable one, because just as he had finished watering the tree and was inspecting the gifts that surrounded it, his grandfather came into the living room with a beautifully wrapped gift.

"Ian, my boy, I have a little something special I would like to give you while we are alone," said Granddad. Ian was excited, but also surprised, as they normally waited for the entire family before opening gifts—and even then, stocking gifts always came first. This was a rare moment indeed.

"I can open this now?" he asked in disbelief. His grandfather smiled and nodded. Ian was over the moon as he hopped up onto the sofa beside him. The twinkling lights of the tree illuminated the room as he began opening his precious gift. Granddad watched with delight as his grandson took off the paper to reveal a red box. He opened the box and carefully unfolded the tissue paper, revealing a hockey jersey. This wasn't just any jersey; it was a Montreal Canadiens jersey. Ian's eyes widened with delight as he pulled the jersey out of the box and immediately put it on over his pajamas. "*Wow*, this is awesome," he exclaimed, grinning from ear to ear.

"I know how much you love Montreal, my boy," Granddad said. "The Canadiens are an integral part of Montreal. Now you will always have a part of Montreal with you."

This was, indeed, an unforgettable moment for Ian. There was something incredibly heartwarming about getting his first hockey jersey from one of the most important people in his life. What he hadn't realized at the time was how important this moment had been to his granddad, as well.

The jersey seemed to glow as Ian gently climbed onto his grandfather's lap and hugged him. "Granddad, you have lived in Montreal for a long time. Who is your favourite Montreal Canadiens player?" Ian had great respect for his granddad's opinion because of the wisdom and insight he possessed.

"Mr. John Chabot," Granddad replied. "He was not only a great hockey player, but he was also a good man and respected by the city. You see, my dear Ian, being a hockey player for the Montreal Canadiens is about more than just winning games. It's about respecting the jersey you wear, and remembering who you are as a person. Don't ever forget that: stay true to yourself and what you believe in, no matter what challenges you face."

Ian smiled, and again hugged him tightly. "Thank you for the gift. I love you very much."

Granddad kissed Ian gently on the forehead, then said, "You're very welcome." Just then, a flash went off. Ian's mom had quietly snuck into the room and captured this special moment in a picture. Unbeknown to Ian at the time, it was to be a defining moment that would eventually change his life's journey.

CHAPTER 9

RECONNECTION

Ian awakened in the front seat of Kate's car to the soft touch of her hand and a warm smile. They had come to a stop on a small gravel driveway surrounded by trees in the early hours of the morning. She had brought him to her family's cottage, located on Lake Champlain, which was about a two-hour drive from Montreal. As she led him inside, she said, "I have spent a lot of time up here in the last few years. When Dad died just over two years ago, this place was like having a little bit of him left behind. He loved it here. I can still hear his voice within the walls. Coming here helped me get away from everything and just think."

The cottage had been in Kate's family for generations, and it was cozy and warm. It had an open-concept design with big bay windows overlooking the lake and a fireplace in the living room. The kitchen was separated from the living area by an island. There was a hallway off to the right side of the cottage, with a bedroom on each side, as well as a bathroom on the left-hand side. She explained that this cottage had been her parents' sanctuary, but after the death of her mother, her dad had stayed away and focused on work.

Kate still had Ian's jacket on. She took it off and hung it on a chair by the island. She was holding the Canadiens jersey. Still feeling the exhausting effects of what had occurred just a few hours before, Ian looked around and saw pictures on the wall of his grandfather with her parents. He smiled as he saw a picture of his grandfather with Kate and Ian on a sit-down lawn mower at 20 Greene Avenue. Pointing to the photo, he told Kate, "I remember that day! Wow, it seems like it was yesterday, but it was so long ago."

She lit a fire in the fireplace, approached him, and softly asked why he had just left so many great memories behind. He explained that the death of his grandfather had left him angry at the world, and everything he loved about Montreal was connected to the great times he had had with him. With him no longer here, Ian was lost, and everything in the city reminded him of his grandfather because he had been such an integral part of his childhood. Granddad's death had left Ian raw, and with such a huge void that he thought he needed to turn his back on everything that reminded him of his grandfather and find other things to fill that void. However, those memories were a large part of who he was, and he couldn't ignore them any longer.

Ian hung his bag on the chair where Kate had hung his jacket. Then he sat down in a leather chair, looking out the window as the fog floated above the lake. The sun was just coming up now, and seeing his reflection in the glass, he closed his eyes and could picture his grandfather smiling at him. So many wonderful memories were flashing through his mind—memories he had tried to forget. He opened his eyes as Kate approached him and gently took his hand.

"I'm still here, now and always," she said. "I understand that the love between you and Reg was something very special and sacred to you. He will always be a part of you, and I hope that I will be, too." With that she sat down on his knee and kissed him.

He smiled and replied, "Thank you for helping me last night, and for just being here for me." He wrapped his arms around her and lifted her up, moving over to the huge sofa in front of the fireplace. As he gently sat down, putting her on his lap, he took her hand and held it tightly while kissing it with misty eyes.

"I never stopped caring about you, and I never will," Kate said. She embraced the moment, smiling back as the two locked hands tightly.

They lay together, silently curled up on the couch, covered with blankets. A few hours had passed since they had arrived at the cottage. The sun was fully up now as Kate snuggled close to Ian. He kissed her softly as he got up with one of the blankets wrapped around him. He went and retrieved his grandfather's journal from the kitchen, which was still in has bag hanging on the chair. He returned to the sofa, and Kate again curled up next to him.

"So, this is the journal of Reg Roberts," she said. "My dad mentioned it in the letter he left me. Dad didn't mention a lot of details—just that it was very important that your grandfather's journal be given directly to you, as those had been his explicit instructions."

"Why now? Why wait all these years to put all these plans into action? Why did my grandfather have the firm wait until I was twenty-five to release everything to me?" Ian asked.

"That's a good question, Ian. All I know is that the firm was under strict instructions. That was confirmed in the letter to me from my dad. Reg clearly knew something that we don't," she said.

"Can I see the letter again?" Ian asked. "We had to flee your place so quickly that I only had time to glance at it. I would like to read it in more detail."

She smiled and reached over him to retrieve her cell phone from a side table near the sofa.

"Do you still have the original letter?" asked Ian.

"I scanned it as a picture and then saved it to my phone yesterday before I came to see you," Kate replied. "Dad gave me the letter on my eighteenth birthday. Also . . . I remember the look in his eyes when he mentioned that the words of the letter were only for our eyes, Ian, if something happened to him. After losing dad, and reading the letter, I hid it from sight until you returned a few days ago. After I scanned it, I burned the original letter as instructed so no one other than us would see it."

He smiled and said, "I should never have turned you away yesterday, as you were and always have been a part of my life, Kate. Even my grandfather and your father knew that."

"It doesn't matter. We are together now, and together we are going to figure this all out."

He put his arm around her as she read the letter from her dad to him.

> Kate, my darling daughter,
>
> If you are reading this, I have passed on from this world, and you are my only hope of fulfilling the wishes of Reg Roberts, my lifelong friend.
>
> This letter outlines in detail what I ask of you.
>
> First, I know things have been rough for you over the past few years. I need you to be strong now more than ever. The firm, our family business, has been compromised, as things are not what they appear to be. Forces within the firm are dangerous and must not be underestimated. You must act as though everything

is normal, because I have taken steps to ensure that the wishes of my dearest friend, Reg, are carried out properly, and they must not be jeopardized.

Second, above all else, you must keep this letter hidden and share it with no one, except for Ian. When he returns to Montreal on his twenty-fifth birthday, he will inherit his grandfather's house and be given an envelope containing a private journal and letter from Reg. You must let him process everything without questioning him, and without revealing what you know from this letter. Your dear friend will need you more than ever after he reads his grandfather's letter.

Third, you must assist him and make sure he receives the items left to him. No one, except myself and Reg, are aware of these items. Long before Foster and Smith became compromised by forces of evil I still don't understand, I kept them in my office safe. The safe is hidden behind your favourite childhood book that you read countless times in my office. It contains a small box of items for Ian. The small key I included with this letter will open the safe.

Lastly, these instructions were entrusted to me not only because Reg was my client, but because he and I were also best friends. And now they have been passed on to you, my dearest daughter. I know how much it hurt you when Ian never returned after Reg's death, but now you and he will need each other, as the events that are about to unfold will affect both of you.

Trust Ian, and believe in him.

I'm sorry to burden you with this. The past can sometimes be a dangerous place to revisit, but I fear now
that it is inevitable. Scan and then destroy this letter
and share it with Ian upon his return.

I will love you always and forever,

Dad

She paused and looked at Ian, teary-eyed. "My father and your
grandfather collaborated to make sure that everything went according to their plan," she said. "This letter was given to me on my eighteenth birthday with instructions from my dad to only open it if
something happened to him."

Then Ian spoke while looking through his grandfather's journal.
"My granddad knew all those years ago that this day would come.
That's why there are all these hidden clues that help unlock secrets he
discovered—clues that only I can understand." Kate nodded, agree-
ing. He flipped through the journal to the Merlinian Elite section.
"Look at this. It says, 'the Merlin Ring enhanced a person's natural
ability, and more importantly, the ring contained the location of the
real Excalibur.'"

"As in, the Sword in the Stone legend?" Kate asked. "I remember
learning about it in my mythology class."

Ian explained to her the truth: how the real Excalibur had been
hidden from the world; how Morgana's life force had been trapped
within the sword; and how the Arthurian legend of pulling the sword
from the stone had been fabricated to hide the truth.

"It's all a little much to believe, but I trust my dad and Reg. So,
what's our next move?" she asked.

He got up from the sofa, leaving the journal with her. He

retrieved the Montreal Canadiens jersey that was still wrapped up and sitting on the kitchen table where Kate had left it.

"What is the link with the jersey?" Ian wondered aloud. "My grandfather went to great lengths to leave me these clues."

"We need what's in that safe Dad mentioned in the letter. Maybe that will help us to figure out what the jersey means," said Kate.

He nodded. "No more hiding and running from what's really happening. My grandfather trusted me with this responsibility. I don't intend to let him down, even if I'm still learning what exactly his life really entailed." He reached into the deep pocket of his jeans and took out a blue felt case containing his grandfather's Olympic gold medal; on instinct, he had tucked the case containing the medal into his pocket the morning he had left for Montreal. He put the medal around his neck along with the pendant he was still wearing. He turned to Kate. "It's going to be dangerous, and I don't know what to expect, but if anything happened to you, I would never forgive myself."

She approached him with a blanket around her, and he hugged her and pulled her close. "We were inseparable as kids," she said. "There is nowhere I would rather be than by your side. We were a team many years ago, and now we are again. Our lives are connected and have led us to this moment."

He smiled as he held her, and she returned his warm hug. Then he said, "We need to recognize the important moments in life, and I believe this is one of ours."

CHAPTER
10

DARKNESS RISING

The Underground City of Montreal is unique. Bustling crowds daily fill stores, restaurants, and bars and hustle to metro stops to catch trains. It all creates an electric and vibrant atmosphere. However, in contrast, deep underground, hidden away from all the shops is a dark, secret catacomb. It can be reached by going through a maze of passageways known only to members of Montreal's Morganian cell.

This catacomb below the streets of Montreal is an eerie, dark place, lit only by candles and possessing a musty smell. Many other major cities in the world—such as London, Prague, Paris, and Saint Petersburg, just to name a few—unknowingly have Morganian cell catacombs hidden deep beneath them, too. Text is inscribed on the concrete walls, while small shelves house ancient relics, including the skeletal remains of dead Morganians who were once a part of dark ceremonies. There are also doors that lead to ancient burial chambers. All of this gives the catacombs a mysterious and chilling feeling.

In this particular Montreal cell, hooded figures dressed in pure black robes were congregated together, whispering, "Is it really her?"

and, "How can she be alive?" One figure stood out from the rest, wearing a black robe with a red-lined hood, indicating that this particular Morganian was of elevated status. She was Abigail Williams, one of three witches found guilty of witchcraft and burned alive during the Salem witch trials. She was a devotee of evil and strong enough to have survived the grave by transferring her soul to another person before her bodily demise. Her life force had the ability to possess human bodies. Many said she had possessed various humans for hundreds of years, never dying but slowing destroying the souls of the human hosts she enslaved.

The Morganian Monks, milling around, cast long, dark shadows on the cold, damp walls. The red-hooded figure was crouched in a corner by herself, talking to a particular shadow. The terrifying aspect was that this shadow moving on the wall was not Abigail's shadow, nor anyone else's shadow; it was a human shadow, floating and moving freely across the walls, independent of a body. The shadow had a voice. It said, "The grandson must have the map by now, but he may be unaware that he has it, or what it is."

The witch nodded and responded, "We will find him before he locates the hidden sword."

"We must not underestimate the new Merlinian, Abigail," whispered the shadow, now walking up the side of the wall and pacing upside down across the ceiling. The candlelight flickered, adding more visibility to the horrifying image. The monks in the room were terrified, but they listened attentively, as did Abigail. She removed her hood, but her face was still hidden by the deep shadows. She was a dark beauty, with straight black hair streaked with red highlights. Her eyes were dark and intriguing, holding secrets only the bravest of the brave would dare try to discover. She was a petite woman, but she had a power and energy that belied her size. The monks approached her as her conversation with the shadow continued.

"My magic is growing, but it still has its limits as long as I am trapped here," shouted the shadow.

Abigail dropped to her knee and cried, "I am here only to serve you, my queen." The room was silent as the shadow remained, moving to another wall in the room. Abigail spun on her knees, following the shadow as the other monks stayed behind her. "I have put another player on the chessboard that will help to retrieve the wizard's ring. Have all your resources available when the time comes." And with that, the shadow disappeared.

Abigail flew to her feet, enraged, and turned to the other Morganians with her eyes glowing red. "I have spent years in the shadows recruiting Morganians and teaching them dark magic. I will be the one to free Morgana—not this new person that she enlisted without my knowledge. I will not lose the respect that I have earned. *I* will be the one in the history books as the person who gave the Morganians their greatest victory in over a thousand years. We must find the Merlin Ring and free Merlin's greatest student and successor, Queen Morgana." Abigail then stormed out of the main chamber of the catacombs as her energy sparked around her, the other followers shrinking back in the dark fearfully.

CHAPTER
II

BEHIND THE CURTAIN

Ian usually loved the buzz of Montreal's busy streets, but on this particular day, the world around him had changed forever. The offices of Foster and Smith were located in the heart of Montreal on the corner of René Lévesque and University Avenue. The incredible high-rise in which the office was located seemed to be made of nothing but glass windows.

Ian and Kate, dressed very inconspicuously, were riding in an elevator to the thirty-second floor. She smiled as she looked at him; he was wearing a vintage Montreal Canadiens baseball cap and holding on to the backpack that she had given him from the cottage. "My dad would be proud to know his 1993 Stanley Cup hat was on the head of a true fan," she said.

He laughed lightly and responded, "Your dad always had a soft spot for me, since I was a Habs fan. I wonder what he would say if he knew I was a descendant of some great king and in the middle of a magical war."

"He believed in you in so many ways, just as I do. And your grandfather wouldn't have entrusted you with this responsibility if he didn't think you could handle it."

Looking reassured, Ian nodded. He also remembered the words in his grandfather's journal: "Trust your instincts, and yours alone." And he trusted Kate.

The elevator doors opened, and they quietly exited. They opened the huge oak doors to the office and went in, Kate leading the way.

The reception area was massive, with a wall of water flowing down as a backdrop to the receptionist's desk, which was currently unoccupied. Three doors gave way to a boardroom with a private office on either side. The boardroom was huge, with designer leather chairs and an expensive-looking table made of oak. The private offices were connected to the boardroom, and all of the rooms had floor-to-ceiling windows, offering breathtaking views of Montreal from above.

As Kate and Ian looked around the office, they noticed it was eerily empty. "Where is everybody?" she asked, puzzled. She immediately headed for her father's office, which was the door on the right. He followed her, but once again he stopped to look at the picture of his grandfather and John Chabot on the wall in the waiting area. He now looked at it more closely, as if he were looking for something.

"Look, Kate, the initials 'RR' are here in the bottom corner," Ian called. He took the picture off the wall and felt around the back, just as he had done with the family picture back on Greene Avenue. There was nothing to be found on this picture, but he was sure it was another clue, due to the 'RR' initials. He put the picture into his backpack. He then joined Kate in her father's office.

Mr. Foster's office had been left exactly the way it had been at the time of his passing. Kate was supposed to succeed him at the firm, but she still hadn't been able to bring herself to clean out his office and take his place. Much in the same way that Ian's grandfather's loss had affected him, so had the loss of Kate's father affected her.

Her father had had an extensive collection of books that filled the shelves in the office. Kate browsed the shelves before finding what she was looking for. "Here it is," she said. *Alice in Wonderland— Through the Looking-Glass.* I can't believe he kept it for all these years." She pulled the book off the shelf and noticed a small keyhole behind where the book had been. She gave Ian the book as she pulled out a key that she had attached to her necklace. "This is the key that Dad put with his letter to me, and I have always kept it close." She inserted the key into the lock, and with a click, opened the small, narrow safe. The contents of the safe included a small box, which she gave to him, and a set of about ten keys on an RR-shaped keychain; these looked quite different from an ordinary set of keys, as some of them were clearly very old. She handed them to him, which he analyzed in great detail. He put the items into his backpack as she closed the safe and put the book back in its place on the shelf.

Out of the corner of his eye, Ian suddenly noticed two people standing in the boardroom looking out at the city. He walked in. One figure standing there was Stanley Smith, and the other was a woman that he didn't recognize. He was confused, but as he went to speak to them, Kate came in behind him.

"Where is everyone, Mr. Smith?" she asked.

"I gave them the afternoon off," he sighed.

Ian felt uneasy, and he backed up to where Kate was standing. "Something doesn't feel right," he whispered to her. "It's damp and cold in here."

"Are you feeling alright, Mr. Smith?" she asked.

"Of course, Kate—and please, call me Stanley. It's just been a busy couple of days getting things organized for Ian's arrival."

She tugged lightly on Ian's arm, as she also sensed something was wrong, and he felt her urgency. They worked their way back to the side door that led back to her father's office. She whispered to Ian, "I've known Stan for years from Christmases together, summer parties, and family and friend get-togethers. He hates the name Stanley, Ian, and always told people to call him Stan."

At that moment, Stanley Smith started clapping as he made his way towards Kate's father's office. What happened next shocked Kate and Ian, and they grabbed onto each other. As Stanley spoke, a female voice came out of his mouth. The female voice spoke with a deep tone that echoed. "Well done, Miss Foster. That was faster than I had anticipated." The voice laughed in a sinister tone. Ian recognized it.

"*Isabella?*" he asked incredulously.

The female voice answered, "Hi, Ian." The image of Stanley Smith shape-shifted into Isabella. "Shifting spells never last long, but it served its purpose. There really is kind of an art to them," she snickered.

"You have a lot to learn, Isabella," shouted Kate. Her voice had also changed.

Ian looked at her, stunned, and saw a menacing smile appear as Kate's eyes turned red. He stepped back and was horrified at her newly disturbing appearance. The positive energy and bright light of Kate Foster was gone, and what remained could only be described as a shell of her former self. Darkness and evil now resided in Kate's body. He noticed that the body of the woman Ian had not recognized earlier—who had been in the boardroom with Stan Smith—had quietly made her way into the office and was now lying unconscious beside Kate.

"So, this is the prodigal grandson that we have been waiting for," said the voice coming from the once-beautiful Kate.

Ian, finding his voice, spoke loudly, "Where is Kate, and what have you done to her?"

The figure with the red eyes turned slowly to glower at Ian and spoke again. "In here with me—for now. I'm afraid Isabella was not as kind to Mr. Stanley Smith, as he's been dead for a while now, and she has been assuming him with a shape-shifting spell when needed."

He looked over at Isabella, who was now sitting on Kate's father's office desk with her legs crossed. "Yes, Stan has been dead for a while now, but that's not important," Isabella said. "I needed to get close to you to continue the preparations. This day has been a long time coming. It's too late for the Merlinians, Ian. They can't stop what's coming any more then you can. The Order of Merlin is dying, and the time of the Morganians is at hand. I'm offering you a chance to join us as we create a new world where powerful, magical beings will rule the earth."

He kept his distance until a force pulled him close to this new Kate. "Tell me the location of the Merlin Ring. I can't keep your beloved Kate alive for much longer, but I love this body much more than my previous host," said the sinister voice inside Kate as she pointed to the motionless body of the unknown woman lying on the floor.

"Easy, Abigail, she's no good to us dead," barked Isabella.

"You presume to give me orders? We have been waiting for this day for a long time, and my patience is running out," shouted Abigail.

The force holding Ian was released, and he was thrown back in shock and fear. After a second of collecting his thoughts, he said to the former Kate, "You're Abigail Williams?"

The evil figure smiled and replied, "I knew your grandfather. Noble, proud, and fearless. But, his heart and his unending capacity to love and protect were his weaknesses."

"Isabella, how can you go along with this? I trusted you, and you are aligned with this witch?" he exclaimed.

"You were so desperate for answers that you would have trusted anyone who could have helped explain what was happening, and that was your mistake. I'm not aligning with Abigail. I'm serving my queen, Morgana, the greatest sorceress in history," cried Isabella, now walking out of the office and into the boardroom. With a snap of her fingers, the automatic blinds closed.

He ran after her. "Please, just let Kate go, she's not a part of this like I am."

"No, but she gives us a hold over you. All that matters is preparing for the arrival of our Queen." Abigail/Kate also came into the boardroom, and he watched in horror as his loving, long-time friend, now a dark and ominous figure, joined Isabella at the head of the table. He looked on as Isabella and Abigail joined hands in silence. As they pulled their hands apart, they created a black pillar of smoke that spun slowly like a tornado in slow motion. Then suddenly, in the midst of this spinning black smoke, two enormous, beautiful, green eyes with thick, black eyelashes opened.

A soft but sharp voice echoed from inside the smoke. "The blood of the fallen king flows through your veins, my dear Ian. We are of the same bloodline, you and I, for I am Queen Morgana, rightful heir to the Pendragon throne and your ancient ancestor."

Ian could hardly speak, but he gathered the words together. "Morgana—but how? How are you here after being trapped by your brother?"

"All in good time, darling." The room was dim, but her eyes provided enough light to see into her dark and twisted soul. "I have been waiting and planning for this day for a very long time—to finally meet the grandson of Reg Roberts, the remnants of the weak and wretched part of the bloodline. I just had to look upon you with my own eyes," she said.

"This is between us," Ian pleaded. "Please, just let Kate go, she's not part of this."

Morgana responded, "Patience, Ian, love. In order for this little introduction between us to take place, I had to temporarily slow down time and create what I call a time lag. Controlling the movement of time was once forbidden—the old rules were against this, of course, but luckily for you and for the sake of this little chat, I have applied my own rules and have now slowed down time from moving around us," she laughed.

"Why keep Kate? Why not just let her go?'" he asked.

She spoke as her eyes revealed a sense of disappointment. "Still so much to learn, my dear. You know, instead of learning the ways of magic through riddles and poems, why not let me show you first-hand the power and magic inside you?"

"I prefer to figure things out in my own time," he said with a determined look on his face. "Besides, I loved and trusted my grandfather more than anyone in the world. If puzzles and clues are what he left for me, so be it. He must have had his reasons, and I would never betray him."

Morgana, with an angry tone, screamed, "I was the one who was betrayed for recognizing that the world was failing and falling apart. Mankind is weak and incapable of creating a strong and lasting society that will survive the ages. People are incapable of ensuring their own survival. It is in humanity's nature to obliterate itself. There are only a select few who possess the strength and courage to reign over the vast empire of Earth to make it flourish for eternity. The time of hiding in the shadows is over; I will purify the earth and create order out of chaos. Join me, and through us, the Pendragon bloodline will rule once more!"

Ian hesitated, worried about Kate. He looked over at her, still possessed by the darkness of Abigail Williams. He couldn't even recognize Kate anymore, as the forces within her were destroying her. It was almost as though for every minute that passed, Kate's body aged and deteriorated more and more; the life force of the witch Abigail was consuming Kate Foster and the beautiful, warm soul she embodied.

"I'm the only thing keeping her alive. I can't keep this time lag open much longer. Once it closes and real time is restored, someone who has not previously been exposed to being possessed, such as young Kate, will not last long. Tell me the location of the old wizard's ring, and you can save her. Be her hero," Morgana bargained.

"I care for her, I always have, but I have no idea where the Merlin Ring is. Please, let her go, and I will find the ring for you," screamed Ian with tears in his eyes.

"Young love—the ultimate weakness," Morgana laughed. "It's amazing, darling. I know more about you than you do. Subconsciously, you know things that you are not aware of—yet." She was becoming very impatient, and the black spinning tornado of smoke was starting to thin out. "It seems we have just about run out of time, young one. Think back to all of your grandfather's riddles and puzzles and what he wrote for you to read. I know he entrusted you with the ring's location; you just need some incentive to put it all together," she cackled, looking at Abigail/Kate.

It was then that Ian closed his eyes and whispered softly to himself, "Help me, Granddad. Give me strength." He reached for his grandfather's gold medal around his neck and held it to his chest. Everything around him seemed to stop, and with his eyes closed, he saw images of the past. Quick flashes of his grandfather winning the gold medal and cherished moments between them—decorating the Christmas tree, and learning to drive his grandfather's sit-down lawn mower—were there, front and centre. The presence of his grandfather felt so real, and it gave him a warm feeling.

He opened his eyes to see a blinding white light emanating from the medal. Everything was still happening in slow motion, but he could move freely, so he aimed the powerful light magic at Isabella and Abigail. Morgana began to scream at the sight of the light magic; it was so pure and powerful that it blinded Isabella and forced

Abigail to exit Kate's body, revealing her wraith-like form, which was frightening to look at. The dark, twisted soul of Abigail Williams was surrounded by black smoke.

Kate's body was thrown aside as she fell unconscious on the floor. At that moment, Ian was able to run over to where Kate was lying and pick her up. Out of the corner of his eye, he saw a wisp of black smoke heading back into William Foster's office, where the unmoving body of the mystery woman still lay. Abigail's wraith form re-possessed the mystery woman's body.

As Ian dashed for the exit, with Kate over one shoulder and his backpack over the other, he looked back to see Morgana's eyes fading, but her horrible scream was still echoing off the walls. He grimaced with determination, and just before he left, he noticed the mystery woman walking out of William Foster's office. Ian turned and exited the office and into the elevator. He hit the button for the lobby numerous times as the elevator doors closed behind him.

CHAPTER
12

THE RING OF AN ELITE

Kate opened her eyes slightly. She was lying on a comfortable bed in a small motel room. It was late afternoon now. She could see Ian sitting at a small table nearby, deep in thought as his mind explored his grandfather's thoughts through the journal. She asked sleepily, "Ian, what happened? Where are we?"

Upon hearing the sound of her voice, he jumped up and was by her side. "Safe for the moment. We're in a motel just outside Montreal. How are you feeling?" he said as he gently stroked her forehead.

"I'm tired, but I can't remember what happened."

"I think that might be a good thing," he said with a worried tone. Kate sat up, and he helped prop a pillow up behind her. She reached for his hand and he took it as he looked into her eyes.

"I almost lost you today," he said. "Imagining that almost broke me, because we have just found each other again. Seeing what we are up against scares me, because I don't want to lose you."

She could see the concern and emotion coming from him, so she responded softly, "We agreed we were brought back together for a reason. So, whatever happened, as awful as it may have been, is part of our journey together. But I am sure of one thing—if I'm here now, safe and protected, it's because of you."

Ian smiled and leaned forward, kissing her on the forehead. "We need to be better prepared for what we are up against," he said.

He got up from the bed, went back to the table he had been working at, and grabbed his grandfather's journal; it now had several Post-it notes protruding from the pages. Kate was much more alert and attentive by this point, and she sat up a little more. The room was in darkness except for a small light on the desk. "How long was I asleep for?" she asked.

"Most of the afternoon. I have been studying this journal for a few hours and have found some things that we should both know."

"I'm all ears."

He smiled and flipped to one of the Post-its. He began to pace the room as he explained, "My Granddad stated that Abigail Williams was one of three witches to be found guilty of witchcraft and burned alive during the Salem witch trials of 1692 and 1693. She was a devoted servant of evil and has an exceptionally strong life force that has the ability to possess other human beings. Many say she has lived like that for hundreds of years, her life force never dying." She listened aghast as he went on, "I met this Abigail Williams today." He approached her again and sat beside her on the bed. He put the journal down and used both hands to hold her cheeks. "She was there this afternoon, Kate, inhabiting your body. Her eyes were yours for a while, but I watched in horror as her demonic presence took over you. I was terrified as you became her—she possessed you, and I was so scared, thinking I was going to lose you." His head sank to his chest as tears filled his eyes.

Kate reached and put her hands on top of his. She was visibly upset as tears rolled down her cheeks, too. She put her arms around him and pulled him close. She whispered in his ear, "What you just told me terrifies me, but I trust that we can overcome whatever lies ahead as long as we are working together."

He kissed her on the cheek and then positioned himself so that he was lying next to her. Kate laid her head on his shoulder.

"Abigail is the witch leading the Morganians with one purpose: to free Morgana," he said. He picked up the journal again as both of them wiped their tears away. "Remember when I told you how my pendant glowed on the metro, and at your place?"

Kate reached for the pendant around his neck and held it, noticing that there was also another larger chain holding Ian's grandfather's gold medal. She listened as he continued, "Gifts given out of love or friendship can trigger inner magical abilities we all possess. My grandfather documented everything in his journal—from everything he learned, to the adventures he experienced.

"I've learned from his notes that magic is a part of human nature, and the trick is to discover what brings it out in every individual. In my case, gifts filled with love are my magic source—that would explain why the pendant and the gold medal glowed when we were in danger. The pendant is a gift from my mother, and my granddad's gold medal was one of his most treasured items. My grandmother passed it down to me after he died, and I have kept it close ever since. Learning how to use, tame, and even harness our innate abilities for the greater good is the challenging task."

He reached under his shirt and revealed the large gold medal hanging on a thick, gold chain around his neck. Kate held it in her hand. "Like the pendant we saw glowing when the Morganian Monk attacked us at your place, the medal also glowed brightly when I faced Morgana, Isabella, and Abigail," Ian said. "It helped me save you. It released some sort of white light that seemed to be created by some of my memories. Something inside me was able to trigger both items so that they could help me combat evil. My granddad refers to it as 'light magic' in his journal—or, more accurately, 'white magic.'"

Kate was intrigued and she responded, "I thought Isabella was on your side?"

He explained, "I thought so, too, but somewhere along the line, her allegiances shifted, and she now serves the dark forces striving to free Morgana. She is also what is called a Merlinian Elite, just like my granddad was. They are the highest-ranking members of the Order who are very well trained, and they act as advisors to lower-ranking members. Isabella has betrayed the Order and is a powerful adversary now." Kate listened as he continued to share what he had learned. "Isabella was wearing a ring—or more specifically, an Elite Ring. My granddad explains that this ring allows its user to tap into the energies that surround us, and it also bonds with the life force of the user, creating a powerful link to produce magical abilities. I think I was able to tap into some of that energy with the pendant and gold medal using my family's memories of love."

He lightly rubbed her forehead, then moved her head off his shoulder and onto the pillow as he hopped up. Walking over to the table where he had been working and reading, he grabbed the small box and set of ancient keys he and Kate had retrieved from the firm and brought them over to her. He opened the box to reveal a ring that looked exactly like Isabella's ring, except for the initials. "This is my granddad's Elite Ring. Look at the silver 'RR' initials glowing on it."

He handed her the beautiful ring. It was light gold in colour, with thin silver strands that encircled the ring, connecting to a silver-and-gold "M" in the middle of the band on the top of the ring. On the inside of the band were the silver initials "RR."

"The ring is so smooth. How were the silver-and-gold letters inserted?" she asked, as there was no discernible way to see how all the letters had been put into the ring, since the surface was completely smooth all the way around.

"I'm not sure," Ian replied. "All I know is, this is the ring that my granddad left for me. There is also a section in his journal that talks about an ancient set of keys that is said to open hidden chambers all over the world. He has detailed maps to some of these locations." He showed her the "RR" keychain with a number of old-fashioned keys attached to it. "But there is nothing here about the location of the Merlin Ring. There is even very little description of it included in these writings."

Kate responded, "Don't you see? This is why you, and now I, are being hunted. The Morganians think you know the location of the Merlin Ring."

"Back at the office, Morgana told me I have been entrusted with the location and may not even know it," he said.

"From everything we have learned and seen, your grandfather went to great lengths to keep things hidden in a way only you can find," said Kate. Ian was now examining the ring. Sitting beside her, he slowly put it on his right index finger, and suddenly everything around him stopped. Kate was frozen beside him. It was as if time was standing still, but unlike the horror and uneasy feeling he had felt when Morgana had stopped time, he felt a peaceful and warm feeling come over him. A bright white light changed the motel room into the living room of 20 Greene Avenue on Christmas morning. He was able to move about in this sort of dream sequence.

What came next both shocked and excited him as he grinned from ear to ear. There, standing before him, decorating the Christmas tree, was his beloved grandfather.

"Hello, my grandson, it's so very good to see you."

Ian ran over and exchanged a long, loving hug with him. This was indeed his grandfather, standing before him as clear as day—but how was this happening? "Granddad, how is this possible? Where are we?"

His grandfather smiled and responded, "We are in one of your fondest memories, and when you put my ring on, the combination brought us together. A small part of my life force is still attached to my ring. As you are finding out now, my boy, magic works in very different ways, and our bloodline is unique. We are able to not only use the energies around us to create magic, but we can also create magic from within."

Ian then asked, "So, where is Kate right now? Is she okay?"

His grandfather smiled and responded, "She's perfectly fine." He continued, "Our life forces were brought here in one of your memories, separate from the physical forces that define the Earth Realm. Simply put, we are interacting with each other through a shared memory." He then walked over and continued hanging decorations on the tree, and Ian followed, picking up a few decorations himself.

"I have so many questions. I don't know where to start," Ian said. Granddad handed him a small Montreal Canadiens decorative ball to hang on the tree.

"Like everything, magic has its limits, Ian my boy. Only ask what you believe to be imperative before our time together comes to an end."

Ian placed the decoration on the tree and spoke thoughtfully, "So apparently, you have entrusted the location of the Merlin Ring to me through clues, but I have yet to find it, and I feel I'm running out of time."

Granddad replied, "Indeed, the dark forces of Morgana are an imminent threat, but you underestimate yourself and the abilities you possess. There will come a day when you will fully understand the true nature of your inner strength and power. Remember what I told you as a child sitting in this very room on this particular Christmas morning. This memory we are in right now has the answer you seek." Just at that moment, Ian saw a younger version of himself sitting on the sofa with his grandfather, opening what would be his very first Montreal Canadiens jersey.

He smiled and said, "I relive this memory all the time, Granddad."

"I know, my boy, and I know my past has put you in a very dangerous position. You are my grandson. And I have loved you from the first moment I held you in my arms. Believe in yourself now, and always remember, when things seem dark and hopeless, find the light that burns deep inside us."

The white light began to fade, and his grandfather's life force began to flicker. "Granddad, please don't go, not yet. I don't want to let you down. I miss you so much," Ian cried, as his eyes moistened.

"My dearest Ian, don't be foolish—you could never let me down. I'm lucky to have been able to pass along such a vast responsibility to someone as honourable as you. I have never been prouder of you. The past was mine, and the future is yours to discover. Above all, be true to yourself." Granddad smiled, and then he was gone in a flash of white light. Ian found himself back in the motel room with Kate.

Time had not passed in the room, but instead waited for him to catch up, so to speak.

"Ian, are you alright?" Kate asked. "You zoned out on me."

Still trying to process what had happened, Ian turned to her and brushed her cheek with his finger. Still wearing his grandfather's ring, he handed the journal to her. "We have to leave. We can't linger here too long," he said.

As she took the journal and carefully closed it, a piece of paper fell out from the journal's back pocket. She sat up to read it as he began to get ready to leave. "This is a telegram from your mother to your grandfather," Kate said. Ian paused and looked at her in shock as she handed it to him.

There was silence for a few moments as he read it to himself. Then he spoke softly, "My mom knew all about my grandfather's life.

She wrote to him worried about my Aunt Tessa, and the decision to pass on his life's work to me." He paused before continuing, "If my mom knew about his life, we need to talk to her. She might be able to help us—but now I'm afraid she's also in danger because of what she might know and can share with us."

CHAPTER 13

SISTERS

Kate and Ian waited anxiously outside the domestic arrivals area of Pierre Elliott Trudeau Airport in Dorval. It was late the same evening. He had called his mother just after reading the telegram in his grandfather's journal. He had been brief on the phone, but insisted that she come to Montreal as soon as possible as he needed her help and guidance. Very much like her father, Ian's mom, Lynn, was loving, caring, and kind. She would do anything for her son, and so she had immediately booked a flight from Toronto to Montreal the same day on the red-eye.

Kate couldn't help but constantly look over her shoulder and wonder if they were being watched—or followed. "How would we even know if we were being followed?" she asked as she grabbed his hand and stayed close. He reached under his collar and held the pendant and gold medal around his neck. At the moment, they were just accessories.

"Both the medal and pendant glowed with white magic when evil was near. For the time being, the Morganians are keeping their distance," he replied.

He held her hand with one hand and his backpack with the other.

He periodically glanced up at the flight information board, anxious for his mother's arrival.

Then, suddenly, she was there, walking through the doors with a huge smile on her face. He smiled as well and handed the backpack to Kate so he could embrace his mom. His mother approached with a small, rolling suitcase. Lynn was a petite woman, professionally dressed, with a warm smile and kind eyes, just like those of her father. She threw her arms around him and he embraced the moment.

"Hello, my Ian, thank you for calling me," she said. "I know there are things that we need to discuss."

Kate smiled, and before she knew it, Lynn was hugging her as well, with Ian looking on and smiling. "Kate Foster, you are absolutely beautiful," Lynn said. She and Kate had spoken on the phone periodically over the years, but this was their first face-to-face meeting in a very long time.

"It's so very nice to see you again, Mrs. Decker," said Kate, smiling.

"You are a grown woman now, Kate. Please, call me Lynn."

Ian grabbed his mother's suitcase while the women walked ahead, talking with their arms interlocked. He followed closely behind, keeping an eye out for danger, protecting the two most important women in his life as they headed for the airport exit and parking lot.

Kate was driving her VW Bug with Ian in the passenger seat due to his height and build, and Lynn in the back. He had told Kate to head back to 20 Greene Avenue in Pointe-Claire. She drove and listened as he filled his mother in on the letter and detailed journal from his grandfather, and how he was now involved in a world—and a battle—he never knew existed. Furthermore, he talked about his plan to find the Merlin Ring and the real Excalibur in order to stop

Morgana's followers from releasing her into the world. He went on to say that his grandfather had left behind clues for him, and that those clues kept unlocking more and more of this mysterious world of magic and intrigue.

Lynn's reaction to Ian's discoveries was not one of surprise, as she already knew the family history and what it entailed; she was more worried and concerned for the safety of her son, as indicated in the telegram Ian had found in his grandfather's journal. She already knew of the burden left to her son.

Lynn was nostalgic as they returned to her childhood home—a home filled with so many memories. Ian opened the door and glanced down at both the pendant and gold medal. Everything seemed normal for the time being, as the objects were not glowing at all. He ushered both Kate and his mother inside. He placed her small suitcase and the backpack next to the L-shaped sofa on the porch. Lynn slowly walked around the house while Kate sat down in the corner of the sofa.

Ian sat beside Kate and put his arm around her and asked, "Are you okay? I know everything is happening so fast."

Kate reached up and gently grasped his hand that was on her shoulder. "I just feel a little off," she said. "I can't really explain it. I'm just tired."

With a concerned look on his face, Ian continued to hold her hand and keep her close.

After a while, Lynn said, "I can't believe the house looks exactly the same!"

"Mom," Ian asked, "you *really* didn't know anything about how this house was being kept by Kate's father's firm, and how it was to be passed on to me?"

She replied, "I knew my dad, your grandfather, had chosen you to carry on his work, but he never entrusted me with the details about what that entailed. Dad always wanted to protect his family, and he constantly battled within himself to find a balance between his family and his ancestors' history."

Ian responded, "Why didn't you ever share any of this with me? You knew how close I was to him."

Lynn stood up and began to slowly pace before answering. "From what he did share with me, his instructions regarding your involvement in his life's work were explicit. 'Let Ian discover the truth for himself, and when the time is right, my words will guide him in the task at hand.' I knew this day was coming, and you must understand—it pained me to not be able to talk about these things with you, but your grandfather insisted we keep the truth hidden until you were old enough to fully understand the responsibility."

"The truth is that Morgana and her followers are very real, and that we are the last of a bloodline that can stop her," Ian responded.

Lynn nodded. "There is more you need to hear, and I'm afraid it won't be easy," she said. Then she sat down beside him and took his hand. She took a deep breath and exhaled, "Do you remember your Aunt Tessa and the years leading up to her disappearance?"

He nodded and said, "Vaguely. I can't remember much about Aunt Tessa, actually. I was so young, and she was always traveling to exotic places. I do remember she and Granddad leaving on an expedition together through Egypt."

Lynn nodded and explained, "She and I were very close growing up. She was my older sister and best friend, and she always looked out for me. We always knew that Dad had secrets and, Mum, your granny, always taught us that everything Dad did was for us. He loved us girls and would have done anything for us, but it was no secret he would have loved to have had a son as well. As the love between you and Dad grew over the years, Tessa became jealous and mean, and this broke Mum and Dad's hearts. Tessa was the oldest child and she felt neglected, knowing Dad had such a special place for you in his heart, Ian, which was misguided, as Dad loved us all in his own special way. In an attempt to try and reconcile his relationship with his eldest daughter, Dad opened up to her and me about his secret life. He was a private consultant that had to travel a lot for business, and this enabled him to pursue his career while, at the same time, combine it with what he had to do abroad as a Merlinian Elite." She got up and looked out the window into the backyard as she continued, "We had that conversation right here, so many years ago. For a time, things were better between Dad and Tessa. Over time, however, she became obsessed with that part of Dad's life and believed, as the eldest daughter, that it was her birthright to carry on her father's work."

"Mom," Ian asked, "what was your initial stand on all that you had learned about Granddad's secret life and the responsibilities?"

She turned to face her son and said, "I was still very close to your Aunt Tessa at that time, and she had confided in me a lot, especially when things were rocky between her and Dad. She was my big sister, and I looked up to her. However, a different side of her surfaced that began to worry me. She became aggressive in nature and desperately tried to win his approval in every venture she undertook in the hopes of convincing him that she was capable of succeeding him."

"She wanted the life that I have now inherited," Ian stated, "She was willing to embrace it. She was prepared for the responsibility."

Lynn sat back down and continued, "Her intentions were not noble, however, and Dad knew that. She was only interested in the power that came with the role, and not with protecting the family's secrets, and the world. When Dad explained his decision to me to have his only grandson succeed him over his eldest daughter, I felt the pain he was experiencing. He knew this difficult decision would cost him any relationship he had left with her."

"If Granddad didn't want her to succeed him, then why didn't he want to pass it on to you?" he asked.

She explained, "He spoke to me about it, but I told him I wanted no part of it after seeing what it did to Tessa, and to their relationship. Even though the problem was between them, it also bothered Mum and me, so we were all affected. I thought our family had suffered enough, and I didn't want to inflict any more pain on us, which would have happened once Tessa found out that I was going to succeed Dad. I often reflected on how family history repeats itself, since Dad told me that Arthur had rejected our family's abilities because of all the problems it caused between Uther and Morgana. Uther just wanted to focus on what he was good at: being a leader of men. And I just wanted to focus on being a good mother."

He took out the telegram from his mother to his grandfather and asked, "Do you remember writing this?"

She hesitated before answering, "Yes, of course. I sent that just after I saw Tessa for the last time. She had come to visit me, convinced that it was time for her to take her rightful place as Dad's successor. I already knew of his plan to make you his successor, but Tessa didn't. She told me that since Dad had told us of our family's abilities, she had been dabbling in dark magic, and that scared me. So, I sent Dad that telegram to warn him, as he always let us know where we could reach him."

Ian got up off the sofa, pacing, before responding. "So, what happened to Aunt Tessa?"

Lynn took a deep breath, and explained, "Your aunt disappeared shortly after that visit. Dad didn't speak much of it, but the following summer when you and I were in Montreal, he left suddenly for Egypt, and Mum was more worried than usual."

"I remember that summer now!" Ian exclaimed. "I must have been around ten years old. Kate, you spent almost every night here, and we talked about one day traveling the world together. I also remember, Mom, the conversations you had with Granny, night after night, worrying about Granddad."

"After Dad returned from Egypt, he was never the same again," Lynn said. "He was quiet and reserved, almost broken, but he still intended to pass on his legacy to you. He never talked about Egypt, and it was only years later that your granny, my dear mum, opened up to me that the purpose of his trip to Egypt was to find Tessa and try to save her from making the most terrible mistake of her life, but it was to no avail. Tessa has now chosen a different path and disappeared from our lives.

"I trusted my dad more than anyone in the world. He touched everyone in his own special way. His instincts were always correct, so I always supported him and his decisions. I trusted his decision to make you his successor, even if it scared me after seeing what it did to our family."

CHAPTER 14

HIDDEN IN PLAIN SIGHT

Ian sat with Kate, still processing what he had learned about his aunt and her desire to succeed her father, as Lynn sat on the other end of the L-shaped sofa. Although Tessa's intentions had not been for the greater good, Ian felt that she was much more prepared to take on the responsibility of a Merlinian Elite than he was. He got up and retrieved the backpack from beside the sofa. He took out his grandfather's journal with all the Post-its marking important passages. He placed it on the coffee table and, returning to the backpack, proceeded to take out the picture of his grandfather and the legendary John Chabot that he had removed from Foster and Smith's office. He then took out the set of mysterious keys and the box that had contained his grandfather's ring. Lastly, he took out the Montreal Canadiens jersey, which was still carefully wrapped, and placed it with the other items on the table.

"These are all the items and clues left for me by Granddad," he said. "They all bear the mark, 'RR,' which, according to him, means they are all connected and tell a story that has not yet reached its conclusion."

Kate looked at him and asked, "What do you mean?"

He responded, "One of the many lessons I learned from my granddad was that initials were a symbol of something continuing, and I believe that all these items are part of my family's ongoing story." He took the letter his grandfather had written him out of the journal. "It all started with this letter. It led me to the family picture that contained the small picture of Granddad and me with my first Montreal Canadiens jersey. The jersey led me to Kate, which in turn, led us to the safe in the firm, which, as you know, housed Granddad's Merlinian Ring and this set of keys. Even though we have all these clues, we haven't put it all together yet."

"Remember what happened when you put on his ring in the motel?" Kate asked softly. "What happened? Did you see something when you zoned out?"

Ian idly put his Grandfather's ring on and quietly noticed that nothing happened this time. He took a deep breath and looked at his mother, and then back at Kate. "It was a surreal experience. I don't quite know how to explain it, but part of me was able to see and talk to a part of Granddad. He explained to me that both our life forces were strong, and that we were able to communicate through a strong memory of ours. It was my Christmas morning memory here, when Granddad gave me my very first Montreal Canadiens jersey."

Lynn had her right hand over her mouth in shock.

"It was so real," Ian continued. "It was like a dream. I have so many memories of Granddad that I have always cherished. Even when I tried to forget them after losing him, I never really could. I spoke to him like I am speaking to both of you now. I still don't fully understand how it happened, but it was Granddad in that vision—or at least a part of him."

Lynn replied, "Your grandfather's secret life was always full of mystery and things that couldn't always be explained, but this thing—this responsibility left to you—really scares me. You know, just because he wanted you to succeed him, doesn't mean that you have to. You still have a choice as to whether you want to do it or not. You have already seen how dangerous it can be, and I'm worried for you if you decide to carry on."

Ian thought for a few moments before replying. "It scares me too but knowing that Granddad went to such lengths to make sure that his legacy was protected, and that he believed in me to do it, gives me the strength to embrace the responsibility. I can't let Morgana be released upon the world. I know how it sounds, but in that vision, Granddad looked right into my eyes with such love and belief that it gave me a sense of purpose and fulfilment. I also don't want to be hunted for the rest of my life by the Morganians in their quest to find the real Excalibur."

Lynn sighed and said, "You are just like your grandfather. If that's what you want, then I support you, and I will help you in any way I can."

Kate piped up, "You can count me in, too." At the same time, she noticed a glow coming from the Montreal Canadiens jersey on the table. She picked it up and unfolded it, laying it flat on the table. "Ian, look!" she said. "The logo on your Canadiens jersey is glowing!"

It was true; even though the ring had not taken him to a place where he could talk to his grandfather again, the jersey was glowing white. Upon reaching for the jersey, Ian could feel a surge of energy running through him, and then the ring glowed brighter. As he moved his hand with the ring on it over the Canadiens logo, the ring glowed even brighter, as did the logo on the jersey, suddenly revealing a map illuminated on the logo. His eyes widened as Kate and his mother came to stand on either side of him. None of them could believe what they were seeing. Ian noticed that if he moved his hand away, the map would disappear. As soon as he hovered his hand over the crest again, the map would reappear.

There was a dotted line that ran through the map, and Lynn, still taking in what was happening, spoke. "Look—the dotted line runs from 20 Greene Avenue to the Montreal Racquet Club. It's about a twenty-minute car ride, and it's located on the outskirts of down-town. Dad left this magical map and path for you to follow, Ian."

Ian looked to his mom, then to Kate, and smiled warmly. "It's time to follow it. Let's go."

CHAPTER
15

___

DISCOVERY

The Montreal Racquet Club is one of the most prestigious clubs in Montreal. Although its primary focus is tennis training, it is also a club for people who just love to play. Ian drove, with Kate sitting in the back seat and Lynn in the front passenger seat next to her son. The three had managed to get a few hours' sleep, but Ian never really got into a deep sleep, as he had watched over his mom and Kate. It now was early the next morning, around 7:30 a.m.

Kate was not looking so good at the moment, and Ian was visibly worried. He looked at her in the rear-view mirror, noticing her pale face and weakened condition and said, "Kate, that witch has done something to you. Have a look at the journal. Granddad must have left something about the after-effects of Abigail Williams possessing someone."

Kate reached for the backpack that was on the seat next to her. She flipped through the journal, carefully checking all the pages that he had marked with Post-its and notes. After a few minutes, she exclaimed in frustration, "Nothing here at all."

Lynn said, "Don't worry, Kate—we will keep searching until we find out what she did, and how to counteract it." After a moment, she continued, "It makes sense that Dad would have led you to the Racquet Club, Ian. He loved tennis and was a big part of the club's development. Your grandfather was a fantastic player, and a remarkable coach and mentor. This club was a big part of his life."

Ian responded as his eyes watched the road. "I remember my early summer mornings on the tennis courts with him, running back and forth, as he always seemed to have the ball on a string. I was too young to realize how special the Racquet Club was to him, but I suppose keeping so much of his life a secret was hard on Granddad, and tennis was his way of relaxing and enjoying life."

Lynn simply smiled. Kate continued to flip through the journal on the section about Abigail. "Still nothing," she noted.

"Hang in there," Ian said. Whenever his eyes periodically looked into the rear-view mirror, he could see Kate's bright, radiant colour fading.

The VW Bug pulled into a large parking lot that was in front of the Racquet Club. It was early morning now—just after 8:00 a.m.—as Ian helped Kate out of the back seat of the car. She held onto his arm as Lynn came around the other side and put Kate's arm over her shoulder. Between them, they helped keep Kate from falling over, as she was very weak. She laid her head on his shoulder and whispered to him, "I need help."

He responded softly, "I know. We just need to find Merlin's ring. I believe it may hold the final answers we need to put everything together, and to get you back to normal."

The Montreal Racquet Club had automatic doors that opened to a huge open area with a reception desk on the left. To the left of the desk were entrances to offices, and to the right, a number of different vendor's boutiques. Straight ahead were massive windows that overlooked eight hard-surface tennis courts, and eight clay tennis courts. The club consisted of two stories, and they had entered on the upper floor, known as the observation level. There were a number of comfortable chairs near the windows overlooking the courts. Lynn and Ian led Kate to one of them and gently sat her down. He had brought the backpack with him, as he didn't want to leave it unattended with all the special items in it.

He continued to hold Kate's hand while she curled up in the huge leather chair. "Mom, where would Granddad have hidden Merlin's ring?"

Lynn responded, "Dad had a purpose for everything he did. If he led you here with the map, then it is here, but I have no idea where he might have hidden it."

Ian opened the backpack and took out the picture of his grandfather and John Chabot. He looked even more closely at the picture and noticed something he had missed before. "Mom, look at this—the inscription on the bottom of the photo." He walked over to where she was standing on the other side of Kate's chair. He continued, reading it aloud, "Men's Doubles Celebrity Invitational Champions, 1978." He handed the picture to her. She looked at the picture and her eyes widened.

"Of course," she said, "the tennis tournament that invited celebrities to team up with club members and compete against each other. Mr. Chabot was very active in the Montreal community, and he crossed paths with Dad because of his coaching and mentorship of kids. He was also an avid tennis player and great fan of the sport." She smiled as she continued looking at the picture. "I watched Dad win that tournament here many years ago," she said wistfully.

"Look at the 'RR' initials in the bottom right corner," Ian said. "Granddad used his initials on clues that he left for me. The jersey led us here, and the picture must be trying to show us where in the club he hid the ring." He smiled as he looked at the picture of the two men holding the trophy together. "Mom, try and remember. Is there a trophy case here at the club?"

"There must be. This is the biggest tennis club in Montreal."

He got up and said, "Stay here with Kate. I'm going to have a look around." He immediately headed for the reception desk and learned that the trophy case was located on the lower level, where players accessed the tennis courts, locker rooms, and training rooms. He headed down the stairs and found it, filled with a number of different trophies. He looked at each one carefully, studying the nameplates. Finally, in the back row of the case, he found the trophy from his grandfather's picture. Many more nameplates had been added since the picture had been taken. Sure enough, the names on the plate for the winners of the tournament in 1978 were John Chabot and Reg Roberts.

He returned upstairs and told his mom and Kate, "I found the trophy downstairs, but I need to get a closer look at it, and the case is locked." He kept speaking as he went through the backpack. "If Granddad did hide something in the trophy, he would have hidden it himself, so he must have had access to the case. He left me these keys, and led me here, so I'm willing to bet that one of these keys opens the case. There's a lounge downstairs. We need to stay together. Let's go." He helped Kate to her feet, and he and Lynn held her on either side as they headed down the wide, sweeping staircase.

He left the two women in the downstairs lounge and returned to the trophy case with the keys in hand. He waited for a moment when there was no one around and started trying different keys in the lock. There were quite a few of them, but one in particular was small and had a round half-circle on the end. It looked like it matched the case's lock, and when he tried it, it opened. He quietly retrieved the trophy and closed the case, locking it again.

The trophy was quite large, but not heavy at all. He was able to carry it with one hand as he took off his jacket and wrapped it around the trophy. He returned to the lounge, which was empty for the moment, except for Kate and Lynn. He placed the trophy on the table and started examining it more closely. Its bottom section was a rectangular block where nameplates with all the names of the winning teams over the years were displayed. Rising up about twelve inches from the base was an upright, rectangular-shaped pedestal with etchings of tennis players in various positions on all sides. Sitting on top of the pedestal was a statue of a player with a tennis ball attached to his outstretched arm in a serving motion. He noticed that the tennis ball was attached with a small screw that could be undone. This struck him as odd, and out of curiosity, he began to turn the screw with the car key until the ball separated from the trophy. It was no bigger than about four inches in diameter, and as he examined it, he found a seam around the middle that indicated it could also be taken apart. He proceeded to turn the two halves in opposite directions at the same time until it separated into two pieces.

There, nestled inside the tennis ball, was a medieval-looking ring with a blue shimmer to it. The top featured two heads facing each other: one the head of a lion, and the other the head of an eagle. They were joined by wings that also extended down and around the sides of the ring. The word "Merlin" was written in flowing script on the inner part of the ring. As with his grandfather's Elite Ring, it was perfectly smooth all around, with no bulges or indentations. Under the ring also nestled in the tennis ball was a note addressed to him in his grandfather's handwriting; it explained that because of Ian's young age at the time of his passing, it was necessary to lead him to the ring by means of leaving clues that only he would be able to put together. Granddad had not wanted it to fall into the hands of the Morganians by leaving clues they might be able to decipher.

Thus, by using all the clues, Ian had found the Merlin Ring. A sense of excitement came over him, and his heart began racing at what he had found.

As he continued to examine the Merlin Ring closely while holding the small note, a voice from behind him spoke: "Hello again, Ian."

He turned and saw the dark figure of the woman he hadn't recognized from Kate's father's office smiling at him; it was the woman that Abigail had possessed before and after Kate. Using her powers, Abigail threw out her hands, and suddenly the doors to the lounge area closed and locked with a clicking sound. "You didn't think I would just let Kate go, did you? A part of me lives in her now, so I have been able to follow your every move since the office incident."

With the ring in his hand, Ian stood in front of Kate's chair. At the same time, he grabbed his mother's hand and positioned her behind him, shielding both of them.

"You can't protect her. Kate's dying, and she needs me now more than ever," Abigail continued as she paced the room. "You have two choices. Either give me the ring and I will release her from my dark magic that resides within her or deny me the wizard's ring and I will suck every last bit of life from her. The choice is yours."

Ian was faced with an impossible decision: lose Kate forever, or hand over the Merlin Ring to the enemy. He remembered the events that had unfolded when he had put on his grandfather's ring, and he thought that perhaps this ring of Merlin's could perform the same type of magic. He looked at his mother, then at Kate, and smiled as he held her hand tightly. He put on the Merlin Ring, and everything around him whirled away.

CHAPTER 16

THE GREAT WIZARD

Ian found himself in the eye of a tornado where winds were howling and spiralling around him. He could see shapes in the blowing winds: images and scenes of his past, as well as scenes he didn't recognize, but ones that he knew in his heart were important. Suddenly, the winds stopped. He found himself on one of the highest towers of what seemed to be a massive castle. He was high up, so he could see the vast forests and mountain ranges beyond the castle and city walls. Small villages and markets surrounded the castle, making up the city of Camelot. Ian was in awe of what he saw, and a nervous excitement came over him.

An old voice said from behind him, "This is where the battle was fought, so many years ago."

He turned around, and there, standing before him, was an older man wearing grey robes and a huge, grey, pointy hat with a blue gem just above the upturned rim. He had a twinkle in his eye along with a long, full, white beard and moustache. The beard flowed down past his chest, and his long strands of hair hung past his shoulders. He wore a necklace that consisted of many different-coloured gems. A brown leather belt cinched the robes at his waist, and there was a sword hanging from it, along with pouches of different sizes. He held a staff with an orb on top of it, and Ian grinned because he knew he was face to face with the great wizard, Merlin.

"It's an honour to meet you, sir," Ian said.

Merlin smiled and responded, "No need to stand on ceremony. Please, call me Merlin, and I'm honoured to be able to meet you, Ian. I know the burden that has fallen to you, and you now have the chance to finally have answers to some of your questions."

"You know who I am?" he asked in disbelief.

"Ian Dekker, grandson of Reg Roberts, descendant of the great Pendragon bloodline."

Ian took a deep breath and asked, "There is still so much I don't understand. Firstly, where are we? This isn't one of my memories."

Merlin, in a calm voice, responded, "Part of my life force is still attached to my ring, so you are able to see into some of my memories. This is one of my darkest—a moment in my life on the Earth Realm that changed everything."

Ian began to pace the floor of the castle tower and asked, "This is where Uther trapped his sister, Morgana, isn't it? You were here—you saw it?"

Merlin also began to pace and answered, "Yes, I watched my two greatest pupils use their extraordinary magical gifts against each other, and I myself aided Uther in his quest to trap Morgana." He elaborated, "You see, there must be a balance of good and evil in the world—the material plane you live on. It is what holds together the Earth Realm we are a part of. However, I underestimated what your family's bloodline would be capable of if darkness found a way to control it."

Ian seemed a little more comfortable now—or as comfortable as he could be, given the situation. He confided, "Morgana reached out to me, trying to convince me to follow her. I'll never forget those eyes, and her scream when I didn't give her what she wanted. She can control time now, and my dearest friend, Kate, has become a victim of the witch, Abigail Williams."

Merlin shook his head with a distraught look on his face. "Morgana's story is a complicated one, and it wasn't until it was too late that I realized she was the evil that balanced her brother's goodness. She wasn't always filled with darkness and rage."

Ian, listening very attentively, inquired, "She was your pupil. Why didn't you stop her?"

"As you are now learning, sometimes things aren't always what they appear to be," Merlin explained. "I learned that Morgana was not only just as powerful as Uther; she was also incredibly brilliant. She was also quite deceitful, as well as an expert at manipulating situations and bending the will of the human mind to hers. She had no regard for the laws of nature and the energies that surround us. I underestimated the darkness hiding within her, and that darkness overtook the once-beautiful light that I saw in her. She came to believe that whatever she could take, manipulate, or use was hers to have. She never respected the power she possessed, and she dedicated herself to evil and enslaving the world to her will. Her powers became reckless and unpredictable. She was always about control, and even now, her power can stretch beyond realms. Those who follow her embrace her beliefs. We must abide by nature's rules of balance; that is the foundation of the Order of Merlin—respect nature and protect the world from those who would disrupt its balance. Morgana continuously disrupted it at will. Stopping time is forbidden, and it can have severe consequences. Talking as we are now, as part of a memory or dream, is not disrupting time; it simply moves much faster than reality. I advised Uther that she needed to be stopped at all costs. He also recognized the threat his sister had become, but he couldn't bring himself to destroy her."

As Merlin was talking, one of his memories unfolded right in front of Ian. Morgana was battling both Merlin and Uther, using the magical abilities within them to manipulate the energies around them to create powerful blasts and beams of light.

"They cannot see us, but you can observe this memory, as it is a part of me," Merlin explained.

Ian noticed the massive sword that Uther was using to deflect his sister's dark magic. He turned to Merlin and stated, "The real Excalibur."

"Indeed. The truth is, for all the power and greatness Uther possessed, he was no match for Morgana—and neither was I. Luckily, when I created Excalibur, I designed it so it could be used as an extension of Uther. In that way, he could channel his powers into it to make it even more powerful than it was, if needed." He pointed at the unusual jewel on his hat, and continued, "Once I realized that we could not defeat her on our own, I put a spell on a piece of lunaniam, which I have since learned is part of a moon meteorite that enhances a person's natural abilities. The spell was to trap her life force—or even Morgana herself—inside an object of great power. The combination of the sword and the bewitched stone was the only thing strong enough to contain her. Lunaniam is also what my ring is made of. I did not possess the unique characteristics of the Pendragon bloodline, so I tapped into the energies of moon rocks to help increase my magical talents. With Uther pouring every bit of power he possessed within him into Excalibur, and with the enchanted stone I gave him, he trapped Morgana inside the Realm of the Sword. The spell on the luna-niam also opened the door to the realm. There are many realms that exist throughout the universe and finding your way in and out of them is sometimes complicated."

They continued to watch Merlin's memory unfold in front of them. Uther fell to his knees, holding Excalibur tightly to deflect the powerful beams of magic Morgana was unleashing with her dark powers. He raised the sword, pulled the enchanted stone from his pocket, and bonded it to the pommel, just under the handle, using a very powerful light magic spell. The Merlin that was part of this memory used his powers to temporarily freeze Morgana. A bright light radiated from the lunaniam rock, and she disappeared screaming into the white light as Uther collapsed.

Merlin spoke softly as the memory paused for a moment. "Uther gave his life to trap his sister. He exerted so much of his energy to transfer all of his power to Excalibur that he left himself in too much of a weakened state to recover. The evil was contained at a great cost. You now must follow them." Merlin gestured for Ian to follow the Merlin and Uther from his memory. "This is how you will learn the location of Excalibur."

The memory resumed as Merlin helped Uther to his feet. Ian followed them closely as they descended the tower's winding stairs with torches on the wall guiding the way. Uther held Excalibur close to him, and they finally reached a dark chamber, which was deep under the castle. He watched as Merlin used his staff to whip up a wind that created a pile of dirt and stone. Then Uther, with the last bit of his strength, plunged Excalibur into it. Finally, Merlin trapped and bonded the sword, dirt, and stone together. All that could be seen of the sword was about one quarter of the blade, with the handle and the lunaniam stone attached to the pommel.

The memory faded, and once again Ian and Merlin were alone, but now they were in the chamber. "That is where Excalibur is hidden, even to this day," Merlin explained. "After Uther's death,

I vowed to protect the secret of the sword and constantly looked for new ways to enhance my protection spells. I wanted it kept safe and hidden from the world, but more importantly, away from the Morganians. I sealed the chamber and created a secret passageway so it could still be accessed, if need be. Then, I used a great amount of my magic to place an invisibility spell on the chamber, so that if it was ever discovered, it would appear to be an empty cave. It has remained hidden for all these centuries, even when an army of Morganians marched on the castle because word had spread that Morgana was indeed still alive but trapped in the Realm of the Sword. I checked on the sword and the chamber many times over the years."

As Merlin was speaking, Ian slowly walked around the chamber. Suddenly, it was as if a movie of the past was being fast-forwarded, as he could see Merlin's memories of returning to check on Excalibur through the years. "The last scene you have just witnessed is the last memory I have of the chamber," the wizard said. "It was only on that last visit that I realized Morgana's power was continuing to grow, and if it isn't stopped soon, there was a possibility that she could escape the Realm on her own."

After a pause, Merlin confided, "I'm afraid, Ian, that our time is almost up, and there are important things you need to know. I added one last fail-safe to keep Morgana trapped within the sword. She can only be released from her prison if someone of Pendragon blood puts my ring on in the presence of the sword. You must also know that this combination will allow the person wearing the ring to enter the Realm of the Sword. I would also like for you to know some of the history of my ring, the Merlinians, and the Morganians. My ring was secretly passed down through generations of Pendragons, who worked with the Merlinian Order to keep it hidden until they were infiltrated. Once that happened, each of your ancestors secretly hid the ring in different locations so that the Order did not know where it was, but they both continued to keep the Morganians at bay as they combed the earth in search of Excalibur."

The vision began to fade, and they both knew their time together was just about up. Ian spoke, "I still have so many questions. How can I stop Morgana if she is so powerful? How can I save my friend Kate? How do I carry on my granddad's legacy? I don't know how to save everyone. I can't stop the Morganians on my own."

Merlin smiled and responded, "You have such passion and warmth within you. As you continue to discover the extent of your powers, you will find more answers than questions, and perhaps we will someday meet again. You and your grandfather had something so special—a bond that is so rare—that it can be used as the light, even in the darkest of times. Trust yourself, and your instincts. Your loved ones are with you, because they believe in you. These coordinates will lead you to the chamber, so remember them: 51.1474 degrees north and 2.7185 degrees west. It's also the place where all this can end. Face Morgana and believe in yourself, as so many others do."

With those final words, Merlin disappeared, and Ian's surroundings began to shift. Only a moment had passed in reality, but for him it had seemed much longer, and he had experienced another life-changing event.

The Great Wizard Merlin, wise and powerful has always been seen as a beacon of hope.

CHAPTER
17

DESTINY REVEALED

Ian found himself once again face to face with Abigail Williams. He used both his arms to shield his mother and Kate.

Abigail spoke, "I'll ask you one last time. Give me the ring, or I will destroy young Kate."

Ian looked at Kate, then at his mom, and out of fear of what Abigail's sinister magic would do to Kate, he handed the Merlin Ring to Abigail. Her eyes widened at the sight of it, and she used her dark powers to freeze him and his mother. Then she walked over to the weakened Kate, put the ring on one of Kate's fingers, and held on tightly to her hand. Black smoke poured into Kate's mouth from her own as she slowly began to re-possess her. At the same time, the mysterious woman who had been Abigail's previous host fell to the ground.

Ian, still frozen, fought desperately to try and free himself, but could not.

Then Kate said with Abigail's voice, "As I said, I won't destroy her, but I still need her for insurance so that you will lead me to Excalibur. Your powers are growing and developing. You have the same unique bloodline as Queen Morgana, but you are still no match for the forces of the Morganians. You are governed by the boundaries of nature, enforced by a wizard who will be nothing more than an afterthought, whereas there are no boundaries for us." Grinning, she continued, "I can see young Kate's thoughts—both past and present—while we are one, so I know you have accessed some of your grandfather's memories. I saw you put Merlin's ring on just now, so you have also accessed some of the wizard's memories. You have forty-eight hours to lead me to my queen, or Kate Foster will cease to exist." With the Merlin Ring firmly on her finger, she disappeared into a cloud of black smoke.

Lynn and Ian were now free to move.

"I couldn't save her, Mom. I let that witch take her, and I couldn't find the strength to stop her," he said angrily.

Lynn responded, placing a hand on his shoulder, "I'm sorry, Ian. The world you are now a part of takes a heavy toll on everyone in it."

He nodded. "We must get to Excalibur—it's the only way to stop Morgana and free Kate from Abigail's control."

Just then, another voice spoke in a weak tone. "She will never let your friend Kate go. Destroying the source of Abigail's magic and stopping Morgana is the only way to free your friend." It was the mysterious woman Abigail had possessed. Weakly, she sat up on the floor as Ian and Lynn walked over to her. She spoke again, "Hi, Lynn, it's been a while. You are looking well."

Lynn gasped, "Oh, my god! Tessa?"

The dark forces of Abigail had left Tessa's body, thus restoring her appearance. Tessa smiled weakly, "Hi, sis."

Ian looked on in disbelief. He managed to say, "Aunt Tessa, you were Abigail Williams's host? Granddad never mentioned anything about that in his journal."

"That's because I lost touch with Dad and he never knew I connected with her life force." Tessa explained. "And it's so nice to see you, Ian. Have you ever grown!"

Lynn helped Tessa to her feet as Ian spat, "You were one with that monster, and now we are supposed to just talk as if nothing happened? My friend's life is at stake."

Lynn gently held her son as he was visibly shaken and upset.

Tessa spoke again, "I know you are angry at me, and you have every right to be, but please let me explain. I promise to help you save Kate and put a stop to Abigail forever."

He listened as his long-lost aunt opened up about her life over the past twenty years. She explained that her decision to choose power over responsibility, and darkness over light, unleashed her deepest ambitions. She explained how balance in life is especially needed for those people who have awoken the magical abilities within them, but she had neglected to consider that. She expanded, "I chose power and neglected my family legacy. I believed that I was entitled to the responsibility of carrying on Dad's mission, but I had this idea in my head that no matter what I did, I would never measure up to what he expected. I also saw this incredible bond growing that was so natural between you and Dad, Ian, and I was jealous. At the same time, I could feel this power growing within me, and I lost touch with who I was. In that moment, darkness began to take over, and I found myself becoming someone else entirely. Dad realized this, and decided I was not fit to carry on our family's legacy, and rightly so. Of course, it took me many years to come to the same conclusion as Dad, and by then it was too late—I had made my choice."

The three of them were now sitting at a table that overlooked the tennis courts, as they had left the lounge from the floor below. Ian was antsy, but he listened as his aunt continued. "When Dad told me his decision that I was not to be his successor, it emotionally destroyed me and angered me to no end. Although he had not told me of his intentions of making you his successor, Ian, I knew in my heart that he saw something in you that he would never see in me.

So, I decided to pursue my own interests. There was an organization that, at the time, seemed like a good fit for me. They operated out of Cairo but were constantly moving all over Egypt. They called themselves the Faces of Ra. This group was about finding, harnessing, and controlling powers that had remained hidden for years. They chose Egypt because it is considered by many to be a source of great supernatural power due to its long, mystical connection to its gods. With the aid of this group, my powers continued to grow. Ian, have you read Dad's journal entries about Abigail?"

"Yes—she was one of three witches to be found guilty of witchcraft and burned at the stake," he replied. "Her life force can possess hosts, eventually killing them. That is how she has lived on through the ages."

Lynn held Tessa's hand as she continued her story. "Dad—who was so well respected in many circles around the world and had connections everywhere—found me. He tried one last time to get me to change my chosen path. He explained that I was at risk of being taken advantage of because I was a Pendragon descendant. Being young and overconfident in my powers, I told him I could handle anyone, or anything. He implored me to choose family over power, but I was too pig-headed to listen."

Lynn stated, "That's why Dad spoke so little about his trip to Egypt."

Tessa continued as if there had been no interruption. "After he left, the Morganians, hell-bent on finding Merlin's ring, tracked me down and infiltrated the Faces of Ra. By then, Abigail was a part of this Order, and I was infused with her life force. There were too many of them for me to fight off. That's when I realized that Dad had been right, and my selfish inhibitions had put me in great danger." She began to cry, and Lynn leaned over and held her sister. Ian's head dropped in disbelief.

After a minute or so, he got up and walked over to his aunt, got down on his knees, and hugged her. She was very touched by his gesture. One of the club's attendants walked by and stopped for a moment, staring at them. Lynn turned to him, smiled, and said, "Family reunion." The attendant smiled and continued on his way.

Ian spoke gently to his aunt, "Why would they come after you, Aunt Tessa? I know Granddad told you they would, but what would have been the purpose?"

She wiped her tears away and held his hand as she spoke. "Abigail can somehow communicate with Morgana, who taught her the art of possession. The problem is that normal people's bodies are not equipped to handle the dark art of magical possession for very long. One of the Pendragon bloodline's abilities is to be able to withstand it for long periods of time—decades, in fact, as in my case. The reason for using me as a host was two-fold. It eliminated the need for Abigail to continually seek out new bodies, and it boosted the Morganians' spirits to know that they had a Pendragon under their control."

"We have to save Kate and stop Abigail," Ian said desperately. "You said you will help us, but we are running out of time."

"I know, and I will," Tessa responded. "I have lived a nightmare for a long time now. I was trapped, and I hated all the pain and suffering Abigail caused through me, but I learned some of her deepest secrets as well." He listened attentively as she continued. "The source of her power is her necklace, which contains some of her torched human ashes. A spell was cast on them by Abigail as she was burned at the stake, courtesy of Morgana's teachings, of course. As a result, she can use her magic for treacherous things, such as communicating with Morgana across realms—and, of course, controlling the human spirit. The necklace is quite powerful, but white magic can break it. Abigail represents darkness, and you, Ian, are the light that balances it. You have already expelled her life force out of Kate once, and that is very rare. I have no doubt that you are able to break the spell and take away her power. She can't possess two hosts at the same time, but as you know, she still has the ability to track hosts she has possessed before, so she will always know my whereabouts as long as she is alive."

Ian contemplated all the information he had heard. A sense of further determination came over him. He was scared but determined to make his grandfather proud. He finally spoke, "Granddad trusted me with this responsibility, but I need your help to carry it out, Aunt Tessa."

Tessa said, "There is one last thing. Morgana needs a physical host to bend the laws of nature and allow her back into this world. Even with her powers at their greatest, she still needs a body from the Earth Realm to inhabit. The Morganians need the location of Excalibur to release her and have her inhabit a permanent host so she can take physical form. She is the most powerful sorceress in history, and if she is free in the Earth Realm again, darkness will cover the earth. The Morganians must be stopped from freeing her, no matter what!"

"Aunt Tessa," Ian asked, "do you have any idea who the host going to be?"

She nodded and replied, "Isabella."

Ian then replied, "My grandfather trusted her. Who knows for how long she has been planning this."

He walked over and sat down beside Lynn, as she had a very worried look on her face. "Mom, I know how much you love and support me, and that is the greatest gift any son could ever receive. I have to see this through, and I know this is a life you wanted no part of, and if you want to go home and stay safe and clear of this, I will understand."

She responded, "You are the most important part of my life, Ian,

114

and I am always here to help you in any way I can. I'm coming with you—and that decision is mine, and it's final."

He smiled, and then said to his mom and aunt, "It's time to finish this where it all began."

CHAPTER 18

THE PENDRAGON SORCERESS

Morgana Pendragon was born to King Britannia and Queen Igerna over a thousand years ago. She was the youngest of three children. Her older brother, Constans, was the heir to the throne. Uther, her other brother, was the middle child. The king's ongoing quest was the unification of the tribes of what would one day become Great Britain. During one of the great battles of his time, King Britannia was badly wounded, and even the best healers were doubtful he would survive. Vortigern, the king's chief advisor, believed he could save him. It was no secret that he dabbled in the mysterious world of dark magic. He was considered one of the greatest mystics of his time, but people were leery of him because of his unusual methods. But even his considerable knowledge could not save King Britannia.

Constans was young and impressionable when he took the throne after his father's death, and he became king with Vortigern by his side. King Britannia had been a very strong king, but unfortunately Constans was of a weak character and not capable of being a good leader, so he gradually succumbed to Vortigern's influence. Whispers began to circulate in the kingdom that his dark magic was growing, and that he was infecting the mind of the new king, enslaving him as a puppet for his plans. Both Uther and Morgana feared for their kingdom, as well as for the life of their eldest brother.

Late one night, the great wizard Merlin appeared to Uther in his chambers. He told him that his presence was due to the imbalance in natural energies, and that the dark magic infecting Constans must be stopped. He went on to explain the uniqueness of the Pendragon bloodline, as well as the magic that lives in everyone that often goes unrecognized. He then offered to train Uther in the ways of light magic because he sensed something special in him that could make him a great leader one day. Since Constans had been groomed to be king while growing up, Uther and Morgana had been left to themselves, and thus they became very close. Knowing the close connection between the two, Merlin offered to train Morgana as well.

As Merlin trained them, Constans became a weaker and weaker king, and soon Vortigern indirectly was ruling the kingdom. Merlin knew that something needed to be done as soon as possible. Although the training of his two pupils was not yet complete, he realized that it was time for Uther and Morgana to unite and try to stop him. Uther and his sister snuck into Vortigern's chambers, and a great magical battle ensued. As Vortigern lay defeated in a corner, he vowed that if he died, the king would die as well. Uther hesitated, unable to destroy him if he would lose his brother as well. Morgana, enjoying the feeling of the power running through her veins, believed Vortigern was bluffing and would say anything to have his life spared. She used her newfound magic to kill the evil mystic. Uther, upset and mortified by his sister's actions, raced to his brother's chamber, but Constans died in his arms, making him promise to be better and stronger than he was.

The relationship between Uther and his sister was never the same, as he felt that she was partly responsible for their brother's death. This led him to take the throne, vowing never to use magic to take the lives of others. Merlin's focus was now primarily on the new king, and he continued to train and guide him on how to control his inner power.

The rift between Morgana and Uther grew larger as the months passed. She still trained under Merlin, but spent more time touring the newly unified kingdom. On one of her trips, she found love. This relationship took up much of her time, but she still remained devoted to Merlin's teachings. Eventually, she was given the greatest gift that nature could offer: a son she proudly named Mordred. However, when he was six years old, Mordred became deathly ill with a terrible fever. Everyone knew his death was imminent, and his mother pleaded to use magic to help save her son. Merlin explained to her that the laws of nature, although sometimes cruel, must not be tampered with. He would not be dissuaded from his belief, and Uther stood firm with him as the boy perished. The death of Mordred changed Morgana, and she vowed revenge on Merlin and her brother, blaming them for letting her son die. Fueled by hate and revenge, she threw herself into learning all she could about the dark arts, becoming incredibly powerful. As the darkness also corrupted her mind, she rebelled against Merlin and his teachings.

She created a fortress deep in the northern mountains where she began to amass and train her followers—many of which she met on her tours of the unified kingdom. Morgana was beautiful, manipulative, and very intelligent, so she was able to influence others she encountered into trusting her ways and beliefs. It wasn't long before she and her followers were ready for a showdown with her brother and Merlin. She was now seen as an enemy of the king because she had corrupted the minds of some of the people against him. She then made a decision that would ultimately extinguish whatever light she had left in her soul. Using a dangerous and forbidden spell, she resurrected her son from the grave. Mordred, reborn from darkness and happy to be alive again, began training under his mother.

The Sorceress, Morgana Pendragon is a chilling, but stunning image of beauty.

After Morgana had been trapped in the realm of Excalibur, word of it reached Mordred. He assumed command of the Morganians, and then led raid after raid in search of the sword that held his mother captive.

Generation after generation, the Pendragon bloodline ruled. They all guarded the family secret of protecting the secret of the real Excalibur, even as times changed. Over time, the Morganians adopted different methods of tactical precision—ones that included less physicality and more strategy, and they fought on multiple fronts at the same time. They put much more serious thought into their plans, and they grew in numbers and power as they plotted for the return of their queen.

Merlin knew he could not protect the location of the trapped Morganians' queen by himself, so he enlisted the aid of a group of trusted allies he had been keeping an eye on for some time. He told them about Morgana and the real Excalibur and swore them to secrecy. This is how the Merlinian Order came to be.

CHAPTER 19

ISABELLA

Isabella stood in front of a mirror in an undisclosed location in Montreal. She was in a large, luxurious apartment, decorated with unique paintings, artwork, and objects that were considered artifacts collected from all corners of the globe. These artifacts and rare antiquities had been collected and passed down through the ages. The suite had a dark feeling to it, but still presented very well. She was spinning her Merlinian Elite Ring on her finger while deep in thought. She had infiltrated the Merlinians, her sworn enemies, and was now second-guessing herself. She was conflicted as to whether to be loyal to her family, or to help the Merlinians, whom she had unexpectedly developed feelings and respect for.

A knock at the door interrupted her thoughts. "Come in," she said. A hooded Morganian Monk bowed slightly as he entered.

"Abigail has taken the girl hostage and forced the grandson's hand," the monk said. "We will have our queen's location in the next few hours."

She turned from the mirror and said, "Does the thought of freeing Morgana scare you?"

The monk answered, "No, Miss Stone. I have dedicated my life to preparing for this day."

"Have my jet on standby and ready to go once Abigail provides us with the location," she ordered.

"Yes, ma'am," said the monk as he turned and exited the apartment.

Once he had left, Isabella admitted to herself that she was terrified. She had lived her life for her family, striving to help free Morgana, and now that the time was near, she knew that it would change the world that everyone knew forever. Fear is a leader's greatest weapon—or it could be his or her greatest weakness. Morgana inspired fear in others, which made her not only a great leader, but also a force this world has never seen. Morgana's darkness was the fuel that fed her power, and with this, she could enslave and conquer the world, as her power would be unmatched.

Isabella walked into her bedroom and opened a safe in her walk-in closet, which was on hinges so it could be swung open. It required a retinal scan of her eyes and a key code to be opened. Once that was done, the door opened to reveal a safety deposit box that was made from the strongest metal on earth: tungsten. She had also used her magic to place a protection spell on the box so that only her thumbprints could activate it. After she provided them, the box opened to reveal a large green amulet with a silver chain attached. It had a beautiful glow to it, and her eyes widened as she heard a far-off voice say, "*Isabella, my love.*" She wasn't sure if the voice was real, for she had never heard it speak before.

She had been young when her wealthy mother, Esmerelda, had passed, and a few months after her death, she found herself lonely and in need of comfort. Isabella's family had been wealthy throughout the ages, as they handled and sold some of the world's most rare antiquities for top dollar. Although always cared for by nannies who treated her like their own, Isabella remained distant.

Her mother's amulet had been passed down to her, so she put

it on. It made her feel safe, strong, and protected. It almost felt as if a part of her mother was still with her, so she wore it from time to time. She had no idea of the true history of her family.

Late one summer night, when Isabella was fourteen and wearing the amulet, her life changed forever. Just as Ian had been able to tap into the life forces of his grandfather and Merlin through their rings, she was able to tap into the life force of her mother through the amulet. However, instead of appearing as part of a memory to her, her mother did as Morgana had done, and stopped time to communicate. The green amulet was a source of incredible power, and it allowed Isabella's mother to visit her on many occasions for short periods of time. When her mother first appeared to her, it was like seeing a ghost. She explained that Isabella had been chosen to play an important part in the return of their greatest ancestor, Morgana Pendragon.

Over time, Isabella's mother revealed their family history to her. She explained that after Morgana's capture, Mordred went into hiding, but created safe houses all over the world for fellow Morganians. The source of Mordred's power came from the green amulet that was given to him by his mother before she went into battle with Uther and Merlin. At the time, he did not understand why his mother would give up such a tremendous source of power before fighting with her brother and mentor. It was only later in his life that he found out that his mother had had a vision of being defeated. So, she gave the amulet to him for safekeeping, and to ensure that she could communicate with him and return to the Earth Realm someday to exact her revenge upon the other branch of the family. Mordred kept it safe for the rest of his life. As his mother had done, he passed it on to his eldest child, and this was carried on through the following generations until it came into Isabella's possession.

The amulet's power had its beginnings when it belonged to

Morgana for so many years. She had spent a considerable amount of time transferring some of her power—a little at a time—into it. Doing this left her in a weakened state until her powers regenerated, but she thought it was worth it since the amulet became an extension of her power, and she could tap into it whenever she needed to increase her strength. This, along with the abilities of magic that her bloodline provided, made her very formidable. She showed Mordred how to transfer power and use the amulet, and in turn he showed his heir, and so on. Each successive owner added some of his or her power until the amulet became a force to be reckoned with.

At the time of Morgana's imprisonment, the amulet had not yet reached the pinnacle of its power, but it was still very powerful—so powerful that, from time to time, Mordred was able to communicate from the Earth Realm to the Realm of the Sword with his mother and learn some of her most evil spells and rituals. He was not able to discover where she was being held, however, as his mother could not see where the sword had been hidden. Abiding by his mother's wishes, Mordred continued to build the Morganian armies by seeking out followers who craved power, without any concern for the balance of magic in the laws of nature.

The details of Mordred's defeat were not entirely clear, but it was believed that Merlin had been tracking him for many years, not knowing his true identity. He finally confronted and destroyed him; it was only then, at that moment, using powerful magic, that Merlin found out about Mordred's identity and resurrection, as well as the way he'd been communicating with his mother by tapping into his memories using a powerful spell. Merlin learned of all Mordred's plans, and that he was the one who had been leading the Morganians. A second person from Morgana's—and thus Isabella's—side of the Pendragon ancestors was defeated.

Isabella, overwhelmed and upset by everything she had learned, continued to contact her mother through the amulet. She learned more of her family's history, and how the Pendragon family had become divided between light and dark magic. She embraced her mother's teachings and unleashed the strong, dark magic she had within her bloodline. With the aid of her mother, she devised a diabolical plan to secretly infiltrate the Merlinian Order and become one of its highest-ranking members and learn their greatest secrets. For many years, she served as a Merlinian Elite, deceiving everyone around her, including one of her mentors, Reg Roberts. What she hadn't expected, however, was that during her training and teachings with the Merlinian Order, her allegiance became divided. Should she serve the light and betray her mother and her family before her, or embrace her family's dark side and free Morgana?

On this particular night, alone in her apartment, something was different. On many occasions, Isabella had been able to wear the amulet and see and talk to her mother, but tonight, it called her name, and the voice she heard was not that of her mother's.

The amulet continued to whisper to her: "Come, child, don't be afraid. The time is almost upon us. You, my dear, have seen and experienced so much in your young life. I can sense your heart is divided, but remember, it was Merlin and Uther who betrayed us and forced our side of the family to do what we did. I know there is much power in you."

"You are not my mother," responded Isabella.

"No, I am not, but it was through my power that you were able to talk to her after her death in the Earth Realm you call home."

Isabella replied, "You are Queen Morgana. Forgive me, my queen."

The voice continued, "I know you are taken with the teachings of the wizard, but you must remember, the Merlinians live within boundaries and abide by his rules. I can take you beyond those and show you the true potential of the Pendragon bloodline. We can create far greater magic from within us than normal people can, and Merlin aimed to limit us. It's our responsibility to lead this world from chaos into order, and we have the ability to do just that, while at the same time avenging the wrongdoings done to our side of the family."

Isabella said, "My queen, I'm proud to serve my family, but with all due respect, you are seen by so many as a monster."

There was a pause before the voice responded, "What is a monster? It all depends on a person's perspective. Some people may see a person as a hero, and other people may see that same person as a monster. It all depends on how they look at a person's reasons for his or her actions. Some will agree that those actions were justified, while others will not agree. Regardless of whether people are heroes or monsters, we—you and I—have the power to rule them all."

Just then, a cloud of black smoke swirled up from the ground, and from it, Abigail Williams appeared, still possessing Kate Foster's body. "I am closing in on the location of our trapped queen," Abigail said. "I am still able to track the aunt. She has boarded a plane for Bristol in the United Kingdom."

Isabella asked, "Are you sure Ian is with her?"

Abigail nodded. "Yes, my sources in Montreal have confirmed that he, his mother, and his aunt all boarded the flight. Leave tonight, and I will meet you in Bristol. Time to fulfil your family's legacy."

Morgana cackled from the amulet and said, "For my entire life I have been underestimated, time and time again. It's doubtful Merlin even knows that I have uncovered a way to escape this wretched prison. You, Isabella, have the strength and power to free me. You are the key to my salvation."

At that moment, Isabella realized that she did not want to have any limits on what she could do, which was what would happen if she chose to be a part of the Merlinian Order. She had felt so powerless growing up and never really fitting in. Her only guidance was her mother, and she wanted nothing more than to make her proud. She wanted to have limitless power without restrictions. It was finally time to be free to do anything—such as destroy the part of the family that had betrayed them.

Isabella smiled and responded, "Yes, it's time to finally regain what was taken from our family all those years ago. The time is here, and I know what I must do. Long live our greatest ancestor, Queen Morgana!"

CHAPTER 20

CALM BEFORE THE MAGICAL STORM

Ian, Lynn, and Tessa were aboard a flight to Bristol. The flight was over nine hours long, and although they were all tired, they were too wound up to sleep. Ian had devised a plan to save Kate and stop Morgana, and it was just hours away from being put into action.

He knew the risks and the dangerous situation that he seemed to be on a collision course with. He was headed into a storm that was over a thousand years in the making. The task of attempting to take on Morgana had fallen to him. He closed his eyes and thought back to much simpler times, when he'd been a child visiting his grandmother and grandfather in Montreal. They had been such happy times in his life, and he had so many wonderful memories of 20 Greene Avenue. His grandfather was always smiling and laughing, enjoying every moment.

He turned to his mom and asked, "How did Granddad do it? How did he maintain a normal, happy life, knowing the burden he was living with?"

Lynn smiled and responded, "Dad's family was the most important thing to him. He bonded with each of us in his own special way. I knew very little about his life as a Merlinian Elite, but I know one thing for certain. His love was something special, as you know. He didn't think of his life as a burden, but as a responsibility to keep his family safe." Ian smiled and held her hand as he looked out the window.

Tessa leaned forward and asked, "What do we know about this location in the UK, Ian?"

He responded in a low voice, while Lynn also listened in on the conversation. "The coordinates Merlin gave me lead to a town in Somerset called Glastonbury." He pulled out his cell phone, opened up a Google search, and read aloud, "Glastonbury is said to be the cradle of Christianity in England, but also according to legend, it is the burial place of King Arthur Pendragon." He opened a map of the Glastonbury area on his phone and continued, "It's in a remote part of the county, but according to Merlin, it was once where the great kingdom of Camelot stood."

Tessa took a deep breath and exhaled.

Her sister asked with concern, "What is it, Tess?"

She responded, "I want to help, Lynn, but my presence puts both of you in grave danger. Abigail tracked Kate after possessing her and being expelled by you, Ian. I'm sure she is tracking my movements, as well. The Morganians have persued this location for years, and now they will have it."

Lynn responded, "Ian was given a choice, and he chose to carry on Dad's task of protecting the world from Morgana. With that responsibility comes risk, but we believe it's worth it. We know what we have gotten into, and instead of running from it, we are running toward it. We are all part of this now and need to do whatever we can to help Ian. We have to trust in our family's power, and our own intuition, just like Dad told us."

Tessa sat back in her seat and warned, "Abigail is dangerous. She's been leading the Morganians for a long time now. They have been combing the globe for the location of the real Excalibur for centuries, and all this time, it never left Camelot. It will really infuriate them that the sword has been under their noses the whole time. Their actions will be ruthless." Tessa paused, then looked into Ian's eyes. "I have never seen anyone fight her dark magic like you did, Ian. She fears you, and she is also desperate to maintain her reputation among the Morganian ranks."

"Desperate?" he queried. "What do you mean?"

Tessa then enlightened them with her knowledge. "There is something more I need to tell you," she said. "For centuries, Abigail's life force has consumed body after body so she could lead the Morganians and carry on Morgana's teachings. Over the past decade, she has heard rumours of someone wanting to challenge her for the leadership, and she has become consumed with rage. Whispers began to circulate that Morgana had an heir, and this heir was the key to her release."

Ian, shocked, gasped, "Another Pendragon? There was no mention of it in Granddad's journal, and Merlin would have shared that with me."

Tessa explained, "Not if they didn't know there was an heir. It was only recently discovered that the heir is Isabella Stone. She is a direct descendant of Morgana, which makes her like us: part of the Pendragon bloodline. Only by being a part of Abigail was I privy to this information. That makes her a dangerous threat."

Ian sat back in his chair and considered the situation. Another Pendragon serving the forces of darkness could break Merlin's failsafe protection spell since the Morganians now possessed the Merlin Ring, and they also had someone of Pendragon blood. He leaned forward again and spoke, "All the Morganians need us for now is the location of the real Excalibur. With Pendragon blood in Isabella, the Morganians can reverse the spell on the real Excalibur and free

Morgana into the Earth Realm. This means that for our plan to succeed, Aunt Tessa, your role is now even greater than we imagined, as our next move may prove to be the most crucial yet."

CHAPTER
21

CAMELOT

Camelot had been the domain of the Pendragon family. It represented unity and leadership in the territories that had become known as Great Britain under Britannia's and Uther's rule. The whole city was a marvel of architecture with the castle as its centrepiece, its towers reaching high into the sky. It was one of the most impressive and beautiful castles ever constructed, with a sprawling city surrounding it. A great wall encircled both castle and city for protection.

The people and merchants who lived in the city were loyal and dedicated to the Pendragons and their beloved Camelot. They had seen much over the years and had survived the many sieges and wars that had served to unify the tribes of Britain. Their devotion was mainly attributable to Uther. In addition to adding to Camelot's lands, he was much loved by the population due to the prosperity he brought to all of them. They considered him to be a true man of the people.

Upon Uther's death, his only son, Arthur, succeeded him, and a time of war engulfed the great city due to Morgana's entrapment and the reaction of her Morganian followers, who loved her for her beliefs that the world needed to be ruled with power. Through a vision, Vivian, the Lady of the Lake and close ally to Merlin, had foretold years earlier to Merlin that Uther Pendragon's son would face the greatest threat to the family's kingdom. Believing this threat to be Morgana, Merlin overstepped his role by interfering with the balance between light and dark by aiding Uther in her capture. What Merlin didn't know about was the resurrected Mordred. Upon the capture of his mother, Mordred kept his existence hidden, but he unleashed an army of Morganians to find and free his mother, and the sieges of Camelot began. Merlin mistakenly believed that these attacks were about revenge for Morgana's demise; he didn't know her son was secretly communicating with her across realms in an attempt the find her trapped location.

Arthur was the only line of defence against the Morganians, but their forces outnumbered his, and eventually he and his troops were forced to flee the city and regroup in the neighbouring villages.

The Morganians searched the many chambers, dungeons, and catacombs beneath the city for the enchanted jewel and sword that held Morgana captive, but none of their explorations yielded anything.

In the meantime, Arthur, with the aid of Merlin, assembled a group of the greatest fighters from the tribes around the countryside. They pledged to defeat the Morganians and serve the new king of Camelot. Merlin knew that Excalibur had been the greatest symbol of strength, unity, and courage in the land, so he forged an identical sword—except for the jewel—and embedded it in a stone near the waters of Lake Avalon, a hidden lake deep in the forests beyond Camelot where the Lady of the Lake would often appear in times of great need. With Arthur's defeat, the people had lost hope and faith in his leadership, and Merlin thought the imitation sword would help to restore their belief in him because of what it represented: unity and hope. The Lady of the Lake, also knowing the truth about the real Excalibur, agreed with Merlin's plan to use the second sword as a unifying tool.

Merlin, still believing that Uther's part of the Pendragon bloodline was the right one to lead and keep Britain unified, told Arthur about the sword in the stone on the banks of the lake. Knowing that his father's sword had been left for him as a sign that he belonged on the throne, Arthur sent word throughout the country that he had found his father's sword and invited everyone to witness him pulling it from the stone. Upon this successful task, Arthur's followers grew in numbers with whispers of what people had witnessed: the sword being pulled from the stone. Thus, his journey to retake Camelot began.

The fighters that King Arthur had enlisted to his cause became known as the greatest warriors in the land. Using the fake Excalibur, he christened this group of trusted confidants, creating his legendary knights. He led a furious campaign to retake their city of Camelot by using the hidden tunnels below the city. Uther had spent time teaching his son Arthur to navigate the tricky maze below the city. A surprise attack from beneath the city and a relentless siege caught the enemy off guard and thus defeated the Morganians. With their defeat and being no closer to locating their trapped queen, they went into hiding. Mordred, the shadowy leader of the Morganians, was never seen in the battle and disappeared. Few knew who he was, but Merlin continued to track the mysterious leader. Because Merlin did not know of Mordred's existence and of his ability to use his mother's amulet to communicate across realms and speak to her, he did not know that anyone else knew the truth about the real Excalibur holding Morgana captive.

Arthur gave each of his knights a seat at what became known as his famed Round Table; the idea was that, because it had no head, everyone who sat at it was equal and united in brotherhood.

Camelot was repaired, and Arthur ruled justly with his knights by his side. Many years of peace followed throughout the kingdom, and his empire grew. When Arthur retook the throne after the defeat of the Morganians, Merlin confided in him and told him everything—how he and Uther had trapped Morgana in the original Excalibur, and where to find his ring upon his death. Now Arthur, among the few who knew of Merlin's secret chamber hidden from the world that contained his personal possessions, could retrieve the Merlin Ring. Also in the box was a note containing instructions how to use Merlin's Ring, and, as Arthur put the ring on, he was able to tap into Merlin's life force. Through Merlin's memories, he actually saw Morgana's defeat and location of Excalibur, just as Ian had. Arthur passed the ring down to his only son, Amr, and generation after generation of Pendragons kept the secret of the Merlin Ring and the real story of Excalibur.

The Pendragon bloodline ruled for several more centuries, but what happened to the fabled city of Camelot—and why it no longer can be found—remains one of the great unsolved mysteries of the modern world.

CHAPTER 22

RETURN TO CAMELOT

Now, well over a thousand years later, Ian stood in a remote, vast open area filled with green fields and hills that went on for miles. Winding roads stretched up and down the hills, connecting small villages and towns. He was using an app on his cell phone into which he had inserted Merlin's coordinates. The area that matched them was just outside one of the villages. Small tour groups would travel by car to Glastonbury to come and see this beautiful region.

Lynn and Tessa approached Ian as he looked around, wondering what his next move should be. He was now standing on the coordinates that Merlin had given him, holding his backpack. He still found it hard to believe that a memory had led him to this location. He knew that Merlin would have hidden the entrance well, but then he thought to himself, *Besides Merlin, only the Pendragon bloodline would have known about the chamber.*

He reached into his backpack and took out his grandfather's Merlinian Elite Ring and put it on. He felt a sense of warmth and protection.

Tessa exclaimed, "Ian, look at the ground you are standing on!"

He looked down, and the grass had faded away to stone. As he walked around, wherever he moved to, the grass would fade away to stone. When he moved away, the stone would turn back to grass. As he continued to observe this anomaly, he noticed a symbol that he had seen before on the stone under his feet and took out his grandfather's journal. "Look, Mom," he said. "It's the Pendragon family crest. I recognize it from granddad's journal."

Ian knelt down for a better look, and as he got closer to it, it began to glow a golden colour. He handed his backpack and journal to his mother, put his hand on the crest, and closed his eyes. He saw a flashback to many years ago, when Merlin once entered the secret chamber. Merlin placed his hand on the crest, causing the stone to move just enough to reveal an entrance beside him with steps leading down.

Back in the present, Ian laid his own hand on the crest. The stone moved, revealing the passageway, and due to the magic of his grandfather's ring, torches set into the wall started blazing.

He then stepped back and saw that Tessa and Lynn were also amazed by what had just happened. Luckily, there were no tourists around them to observe what had just taken place. He took his backpack and journal from his mother and stepped onto the stairs, which were made of solid rock and descended down about sixteen feet. His mother and Aunt Tessa followed closely behind. After a long descent into flame-lit darkness, the three found themselves in an open chamber; the three stood there, looking at a number of large rectangular stone boxes scattered throughout. They had found their way into an ancient medieval burial chamber.

CHAPTER 23

THE LOST CHAMBER OF EXCALIBUR

Ian blew away the dirt and dust that had collected on the ancient rectangular boxes over the years and began to study them. Lynn and Tessa slowly made their way around the chamber, taking in their surroundings. It was a circular chamber, and the stone boxes turned out to be sarcophagi. The walls of the chamber were filled with etchings and drawings, including battles that had taken place in the past. Ian could make out a particularly beautiful etching of Camelot.

He now turned his attention back to the sarcophagi. He said, "These are the final resting places of the earlier Pendragons. Look at some of the names here" As he walked around the chamber, he started reading aloud the names that were written and carved so beautifully onto each sarcophagus:

King Britannia Pendragon – High King of Britain

Queen Igerna Pendragon – Wife to Britannia and beloved mother of Constans, Uther, and Morgana

King Constans Pendragon – Eldest son of Britannia and Igerna

Queen Igraine Pendragon – Wife to Uther and
beloved mother of Arthur

As he approached the final sarcophagus, he noticed that it read,

King Uther Pendragon – Son of Britannia and Igerna
and Father to Arthur

Each coffin also displayed the royal crest of the Pendragon. As
Ian approached the final resting place of Uther Pendragon, the crest
on his particular sarcophagus glowed a golden colour. As he moved
his hand over the crest, his grandfather's ring began to glow more
brightly, and the sarcophagus's enormous stone cover slid aside.
His eyes widened as he looked inside the open box. There were
no remains of the great king; instead, it was another entrance to a
chamber below, with a winding staircase descending still deeper
into the ground. Once again, the movement of the sliding stone had
caused all the torches to ignite down the spiral staircase. Tessa and
Lynn slowly approached the now-open sarcophagus. Ian stepped
up and into the open sarcophagus, then carefully found his footing
on the first step. He turned and helped his mother and aunt get up
and in.

The staircase wound downwards, and cobwebs hung like blankets as he brushed them aside, making his way deeper and deeper
underground. He finally reached the bottom of the stairs, which
led into another large chamber. At first glance, the chamber looked
empty, like a deserted cave. He recognized the empty chamber, as it
was the same one Merlin had showed him from his memory.

Ian felt a sense of cold fall over him as he stopped, unsure
to proceed. Something was off, and suddenly, a cloud of black
smoke spiralled up from the ground to reveal Abigail Williams in
Kate's body.

"Well done, Ian, well done indeed," she said.

He asked, "Is Kate still alive?"

Abigail laughed. "Young Katherine is a fighter, and I can still feel her soul in here with me, so yes, she's still alive." He noticed she was wearing the Merlin Ring, but it was not glowing. He continued to listen as she spoke again, "We have come all this way and waited so long to find our queen."

"Look around, witch, the room is empty," Ian replied. "You have achieved nothing."

Abigail, now pacing the empty cave, spoke again with a sinister smile. "I can hear her screaming, you know. With each passing minute, Kate Foster inches closer to death."

Ian dashed forward in anger, but Tessa held him back by grabbing his hand. "Patience, Ian. Just a little longer," she whispered.

Abigail once again spoke as she continued to pace around Ian, Tessa, and Lynn. "Hi, Tessa. How are you keeping, sister? We *were* like sisters, you know. We experienced so much together. Such a special bond sisters have—don't you think, Lynn?"

"You stole Tessa from us, and you know nothing about a sisterly bond," Lynn growled. "You kill and hurt people, and you take without conscience. That's not a bond—it's just evil trickery, and abuse of power. You are nothing more than a mere thief who takes what isn't hers to have."

Abigail, now visually upset, spat as her eyes glowed red, "I was more of a sister to Tessa than you ever were. I let her unleash the power within her."

Lynn walked closer to Tessa and said, "You used your dark magic on Tessa because she is special: a Pendragon. Love and sisterhood are about letting each person make her own decisions, and the others supporting that decision. All that matters now is that Tessa is standing here with us against you."

Tessa turned to Lynn and smiled brightly, and then to Abigail, with a look of hatred and defiance.

Abigail responded impatiently, "Enough of this useless chatter. Where is Morgana being held captive in this cave? Tell me, Ian, my patience is up, and your beloved Kate is out of time."

"Wait," Ian cried. "I need the Merlin Ring, Abigail. Only a Pendragon together with the ring can lift the protection spell on this chamber and reveal its secret."

Abigail's sinister smile once again took form, and she laughed and said, "Well, lucky for me, I have someone who can do just that." Out of the corner of his eye, he saw someone coming down the stairs. When the figure came out of the shadows, it was Isabella Stone.

"Hello, Ian, my dear," she greeted. "There's nothing better than a family reunion well over a thousand years in the making."

CHAPTER
24

RECONCILIATION

Tessa continued to hold Ian back. He slipped off his grandfather's ring and gave it to Tessa, as part of their plan they had discussed on the plane.

Isabella slowly approached, making direct eye contact with him and said, "Your grandfather was a remarkable man. I learned so much from him, including the importance of family."

He responded, "We are all part of the same family. Don't you see that? Morgana divided our family for her own personal gain. We are all just pawns in her chess game to reclaim her place here on Earth and destroy the world we know."

"We may share the same bloodline, but we have different beliefs," Isabella replied. "Morgana became an outcast for wanting to save her son's life."

He shook his head as he responded loudly, "She has corrupted your thinking. Some decisions aren't ours to make. Life and death are a part of nature's cycle. It's not for us to decide who lives and who dies. I have learned this, just as you should have. Do you not think for a minute that I wouldn't do anything to be with my granddad again? Just because we have the ability to defy nature does not mean we have the right to for our own selfish purposes. That's what makes life so extraordinary and precious. Enjoy the moments of your life, for you never know when they will end."

Isabella, now frustrated, made her way towards Abigail while still focusing on Ian. "You don't know what it's like to be told that you alone are the only hope of saving your family," she said. "I can save our queen and restore her freedom that was taken from her all those years ago."

Ian tried reasoning with her by saying, "Believing that Morgana's freedom is the key to saving your family's honour is madness. She will devour you, and anything else that stands in her way."

At that moment, Abigail began to slowly hunch over, and then she fell to her knees. "What is happening to me?" she exclaimed, looking at Isabella.

Tessa, now wearing her father's Elite Ring, was reciting a spell. It caused the ring to glow brightly, and white smoke started slowly swirling around her while still keeping her visible. She turned to her sister and explained, "This has to be the plan, sis. You don't serve the darkness for all those years as I did without learning a few tricks. Whatever happens, you must not blame Ian. We will only get one chance at this. Even through all the years we were separated, I never stopped loving you or the family. I have to do this to make up for the pain and suffering I caused all of you for so many years."

Lynn nodded with tears running down her cheeks. "Thank you, Tessa," she sobbed. "I love you, too."

Suddenly, the black smoke that was Abigail's life force poured out of Kate's mouth. Ian ran to Kate's aid, who was now herself once again, but lying unconscious. He carefully held her in his arms and stroked her forehead gently. She was still breathing, but very weakly. He took off the light jacket he was wearing and wrapped it around her. He then took the Merlin Ring off her finger and gently laid her in a corner of the chamber, away from danger. Tessa had now compelled Abigail Williams's life force back into her body by taking the black smoke that had poured from Kate's mouth into her own, and the magical spell Tessa had concocted was now holding Abigail hostage inside her.

Isabella, who was standing between Ian and his Aunt Tessa, created a bright white light, trying to blind him so that she could take the Merlin Ring from him. However, he had already put it on. He raised his hand, pointing it at her, as it began to glow dazzlingly. Suddenly, her magic was deflected back, temporarily blinding and freezing her.

Ian approached his aunt and spoke softly, "Aunt Tessa, you must let her out. It's the only way."

Lynn implored, "Tessa, please fight, my sister—don't let her consume you."

Ian closed his eyes and thought of a memory he had of his grandfather and himself on his sit-down lawnmower and smiled. These memories with his grandfather were a source of such great strength for him, and combined with the Merlin Ring, created an incredible amount of magical energy. The ring continued to glow, and he could feel a surge of power within him. His eyes were now beaming white, and a white glow also surrounded his body.

Tessa was now screaming, "Ian, it hurts, I can't hold her, she's ripping through me!"

Ian shouted, "Release her, Aunt Tessa, I'm ready."

Tessa continued to scream as Lynn held her hand. Her eyes turned red as she threw Lynn's hand away. Abigail was back in control.

Using every ounce of the strength from the combination of the ring and one of his fondest memories, Ian froze the possessed Tessa Roberts. His power was so immense at the moment that even Abigail's life force was frozen, too. The necklace that had the charm containing her ashes was visible around Tessa's neck; it was a part of Abigail, following and appearing on whoever's body she was inhabiting. Since this was the source of Abigail's power, Ian used his new-found strength and extended his arm in its direction. The Merlin Ring seemed to attract it, and the necklace flew off her neck and into his hand. His eyes were still white, but he looked at his mother as he knelt down on one knee. "Aunt Tessa said this is our only chance, Mom," he said.

Lynn left Tessa's side, approached him, and responded, "Your aunt has sacrificed herself to save us. Make her proud."

With tears rolling down his face, Ian closed his hand around the charm, and suddenly it burst into flames. Smoke poured out of his clenched fist, and when he opened it, a small orange flame flicked about ten inches tall in the palm of his hand. The charm melted in his hand, and Abigail's essence began to burn. She screamed in agony as she unfroze. The flame in his hand turned white, and the ashes dissolved into the air. A simultaneous scream filled the air as both Abigail and Tessa burned in a white fire that engulfed every bit of them.

The white glow faded from Ian's eyes, and his brown eyes returned to normal. The chamber was quiet once again, but it had changed in appearance. He opened his eyes to find his mother still beside him, and he also turned around to make sure Kate's unconscious body was still visible. Ian and Lynn hugged each other, both of them crying. There was nothing left from the fire, but as Lynn turned from the hug, she noticed her father's ring on the ground. She picked it up, and Ian gently closed his mother's hand around it and smiled.

"You keep this safe," he said.

Lynn took the ring, weeping, overwhelmed with loss.

The spell that had temporarily blinded and frozen Isabella

had now worn off. Her eyesight had returned just as Tessa's body exploded and Abigail Williams was vanquished.

As Isabella approached Ian and Lynn, he told her, "That's what it means to be family. Do you really think Morgana would sacrifice herself to save you, Isabella?"

Ian was still in tears as he said, "My aunt gave her life to stop that witch and the evil she inflicted upon so many."

He then rushed over to check on Kate, and she woke up to the soft touch of his hand on her cheek. She spoke softly, "You saved me, Ian. She's gone. I don't have that awful feeling in the pit of my stomach anymore. I feel like I have just woken up from a terrible nightmare."

Ian picked her up and made his way over to Lynn. The chamber that once looked empty was now full of various historical items. The Merlin Ring had lifted the protection spell that kept the true surroundings of the chamber hidden and safe. There were holes in the walls containing many scrolls, much like the Merlinian temple in Montreal. Different artifacts were neatly organized in piles on the floor. At the centre of the chamber were four cylindrical pillars that stretched high to the ceiling with text carved on them. The text was not English, but as Ian moved his hand with the ring on it over the mysterious text, it changed to English, and he could read them.

Isabella nervously approached, unsure of her place now. "Merlinian teachings say that only the Pendragon bloodline can wield the many powers contained within his ring," she said.

Ian, suspicious of Isabella's motives, now stayed a distance from her.

Between the pillars were sets of stairs leading up to a central, circular platform. Here, a single stone sarcophagus sat in front of a huge pile of stones that housed the real Excalibur. Surrounding the circular platform were life-sized statues of kneeling knights, all holding their swords with the tips in the ground in front of them.

There were gaps between the statues so one could approach the sarcophagus and Excalibur. There was also a small statue of a man with a sword kneeling on top of the stone sarcophagus. This particular sarcophagus was beautifully carved, with intricate details on the cover.

Isabella made her way up the stairs to where Ian was now standing, still holding Kate. He sat her up against one of these mighty stone knights. He moved his hand with the Merlin Ring across a line of text on the sarcophagus cover and read, "This is the final resting place of the mighty Uther Pendragon. May he forever guard the sword in the stone." He slowly approached Excalibur, which was embedded deep in the stone behind the sarcophagus. He could not believe that, with his own eyes, he was looking through the entrapment charm created by Merlin: the only thing keeping Morgana Pendragon from returning to the Earth Realm.

The Chamber of Excalibur - hidden from the world, this chamber contains the original Excalibur used to defeat and trap the sorceress Morgana.

CHAPTER 25

THE GRANDSON'S CHOICE

Ian, still emotional from the events of Tessa's sacrifice, looked on in amazement at the real Excalibur that was half-buried in stone. He exclaimed excitedly, "Aunt Tessa would have loved to have seen this, Mom." But he didn't hear a response from his mother; only a nervous whimper. As he turned to her, he looked on in shock as Isabella now held his mom hostage, with two small daggers at her neck. Isabella was not actually holding the knives; instead, they were floating in mid-air against Lynn's neck.

Isabella walked towards him and said, "Please, give me the wizard's ring. I don't want to hurt your mother."

Ian replied, "If only my grandfather could see you now. He trusted you to guide and protect me. Now you are betraying everything he stood for, as well as threatening his daughter's life?"

"There are things you don't understand," she responded. "The burden of being a Pendragon can haunt your every move and dictate your every action. I loved your grandfather and everything he stood for, and I believe you are capable of extraordinary things. But alas, I was born on the wrong side of the family tree, and I have come to terms with that. We are at the point in time where I must fulfil my family's duty. I am the last descendant of Mordred, son of Morgana, and I must avenge my ancestors. However, I will leave this next decision to you."

He asked, "What decision are you talking about?"

"You have a choice to make," Isabella answered. "The Merlin Ring on a Pendragon finger is the only thing that will reveal the release spell and free Morgana. Also, this spell will allow the Pendragon wearing the ring access to Morgana's prison. That means either you, me, or your mother must enter the Realm of the Sword and remain there while Morgana re-enters the Earth Realm. This much I've learned over the years, being a descendant of Morgana. It is your choice as to whom that person will be."

"Isabella, listen to me. Together we might be able to end this," Ian pleaded. "Our combined powers might be enough to destroy the release spell on the charm and trap Morgana forever."

Isabella shook her head. "I've done horrible things, but I chose my path, and I now accept that. There's no going back from the things I've done, and now I have to live with them and continue on that path."

"I will be the one to go in," Ian declared.

"I do admire your courage, and if it makes any difference, your grandfather would be proud," said Isabella.

Lynn cried out in anguish, "Please, Ian, don't do this! You will be giving Morgana exactly what she wants."

He inched closer to Lynn, with the knives still floating in the air at her throat.

"Careful, Ian, no tricks," warned Isabella.

He stopped and looked his mother in the eye. "This is what Granddad asked of me," Ian said. "The letter that brought me into this magical world our family is a part of—and everything that happened afterwards—has all led to this moment. I have to try to stop her, Mom."

Lynn opened her hand and placed her father's ring on his finger.

He was now wearing both the Merlin Ring and his grandfather's Elite Ring.

Isabella laughed and informed him, "You are no match for Morgana. She will extinguish your life force and appropriate your body. The Realm of the Sword has been her domain for over a thousand years, and you are walking into her lair."

Embracing his mother, he said, "No matter what happens, I will always be with you. Please look out for Kate. I love you."

She returned the embrace, and whispered, "I love you very much. I could not have asked for a better son."

With his mother in tears, Ian turned away and approached Kate. He knelt down in front of her and said, "If there is one thing I have learned from all this, it's that the love of family and friends is truly something special. I know we have only just found each other again, but you have always believed in me, and now it's time for me to live up to that belief. It's time for me to carry on my grandfather's greatest responsibility—not just the protection of our family, but also of the world. In case I don't make it back, I want you to know that I care for you very much." With that being said, he kissed her as she put her arms around him and held him tightly.

She did not want to let go, but she was too weak to hold on any longer as she cried softly. She whispered in his ear, "I care for you, too. Please, please find a way back to me."

He reluctantly pulled away and approached the sword in the stone. He had his grandfather's ring on his right hand, and the Merlin Ring on his left. He waved his left hand over the enchanted stone on Excalibur, and it began to shake and glow a bright blue colour. The ancient release spell was inscribed on the sword, and the text began to shimmer in gold. Once again, as he placed his hand in close proximity to the verse, it changed to modern English. With his palm down against the charm, he read aloud, "The hand of magic contains within it the energies to unlock the gateway of the fabric that divides the realms of the universe, giving way to the realm beyond realms."

Suddenly, the blue light emanating from the stone froze him and turned his eyes white. His life force began its journey to a different plane of existence while his body remained tethered to Excalibur.

CHAPTER 26

THE REALM OF THE SWORD

Ian felt as though he were descending into a vortex. He was terrified as he continued to fall downward, farther and farther. He soon realized that the vortex was actually the passageway that connected the Earth Realm to the Realm of the Sword. He couldn't see where he was going, nor was he able to control the rate of descent as he continued to fall into a dark abyss. There were many other realms adjacent to the maelstrom, but there seemed to be a barrier between it and all of them. He could hear the screams of trapped souls coming from the other realms and see frightening apparitions trying to grab and hold on to him. His eyes were wide open in terror as he witnessed the horrific appearances of these agonized spirits around him, even though they could not penetrate the barrier.

Finally, his descent began to slow, and he eventually found himself on a floating platform made of stone. As he found the strength to get to his feet, he took in his surroundings. There were many other smaller platforms floating around the larger one he was on. All of them, including the one he was standing on, looked like large portions of land had been ripped from the earth and were now floating freely. Space also seemed infinite with no ground in sight: just a chasm of darkness above and below the island platforms. The one he stood on was circular in shape with large columns standing throughout, holding up a roof. A winding staircase was at the centre of the platform, which made its way to the upper level, or roof area, high above.

As he made his way toward the stairs, he stopped to examine rows and rows of orbs that were sitting on small stone stands. As he peered into some of them, he could clearly see the events taking place within them. He looked into one particular orb and saw one of his many memories with his grandfather, which gave him a chilling, eerie feeling. As he looked around at the different images, he thought to himself, *These orbs contain memories, and not just mine. What would Morgana want with so many memories, and how did she get them?* He recognized Merlin, Uther, and Morgana in some of the orbs. Confused by what he saw, he made his way to the staircase and began climbing.

As he ascended, he found himself in a dark, candlelit stairwell that led to the circular roof of a tower that was attached to the circular platform he had arrived on; this tower structure looked like part of the fortress Morgana had occupied when she was living in the Earth Realm. As he reached the roof, huge flames ignited in caldrons along the edges. The winds began to pick up, thunder could be heard, and lightning could be seen, as if a storm were raging on in the darkness above. In the centre of the roof were four sets of stairs that rose in the shape of a pyramid. They led up to a large stone throne sitting on a dais, ancient and medieval in design, that looked out over the Realm of the Sword.

He slowly approached the stairs toward the back of the throne and walked halfway up. Suddenly, the throne began to slowly turn, revealing a stunning woman dressed in black sitting with her legs crossed. "Well, well, well, if it isn't the grandson, Ian Dekker!" she said.

As the throne came to a stop, Ian finally came face to face with Morgana. She appeared to be a woman in her mid-forties, and she looked as though she had not aged at all since entering her prison. She was a sight to behold, with her beauty contrasted by a sinister smile. Her long dress was black, shimmery, and had a black belt with a detailed skull buckle that looked like a very detailed ornament. The dress had slits on both sides that revealed a glimpse of her legs. A black, red-lined cape hung over her shoulders, and her black boots went to mid-calf and were laced all the way up. Multiple rings adorned every finger. Her black hair was long and flowing. Her face was inscrutable, with red lipstick accentuating her lips and mouth. Her green eyes glowed with an intensity that was captivating. Ian was forced to admit that even though she might be the most malevolent and powerful woman ever born, she was also incredibly attractive.

She began to clap as she laughed, "Bravo, my dear Ian, bravo. Although our last chat was cut short, I knew you would find your way here. You are just as brave as you are foolish, and I was counting on that. I knew the grandson of Reg Roberts would choose to journey here in the name of the Pendragon legacy."

"Well you know, I had heard so much about you, and after our first chat, I decided I just couldn't pass up a chance to meet the great Morgana," he responded.

She uncrossed her legs and stood up with a snicker. "The pleasure is indeed all yours," she told him. "I have been planning this moment for a very long time. Leading you down a path you didn't even know existed. Everything you have encountered on your journey was all carefully orchestrated by me to ensure you would be here now, standing before me." She slowly walked down the stairs to where he was standing, staring him in the face. "You are indeed handsome, and perhaps under different circumstances, we could have ruled together."

Morgana Pendragon sitting on her throne in the Realm Of The Sword.

He replied, "You may have used your powers of seduction to manipulate other men, but that tactic won't work with me. You have convinced so many people to follow you even though what you are doing is wrong. How many people must you continue to deceive simply for your own selfish goals?"

"Deceive, you say?" she cried. "I'm the only one who truly recognizes and understands the strength and responsibility of our bloodline."

He replied, "You can tell yourself whatever you need to in order to justify your actions, but you had the potential to use all of your power for good, and you chose to use it for evil."

She leaned in toward him. His heart was now pounding in his chest. "Such a brave and noble young man you are. Men and women alike have trembled at my feet, but not you." His eyes followed her as she moved around him and said, "I once thought as you did. You believe you serve a greater purpose and respect the laws of nature, even when you have the ability to change nature for the better. We are unique in our ability to create power from within, so the limits of nature do not apply to us. Why would we be given such gifts if not to change the world around us for the better?"

She slowly walked past him down the stairs and looked out into the dark abyss, where lightning provided the only source of brightness. The winds picked up and began to blow the rain that had now started to fall. She continued, "This prison I was sentenced to has been my awakening. Trapped here for centuries by my beloved brother, who was corrupted by Merlin, only confirmed to me that the decision I made all those years ago was the correct one." She turned and looked at him, smiling again as she expanded, "Our ancestry's very nature can give birth to incredible magic, and I have discovered a way to harness much power for myself."

"What do you mean?" he queried.

She explained, "Memories, Ian, memories. With our innate ability to use powerful family heirlooms, we can harness the ultimate power: memories."

Ian remembered that he had indeed used his memories to create white magic. Even now, he was wearing his grandfather's gold medal and the pendant from his mom around his neck, along with both his grandfather's and Merlin's rings.

Morgana continued, "You don't honestly believe that harnessing the power of memories was specific to you—do you? You see, before my banishment to this place, I left an amulet with some of my power in it with my only son, Mordred. The wizard let him die right before my eyes, even though Merlin had the power to defy death. My brother stood by as his sister, a mother, watched nature rip her child from her. At that moment, I became something else entirely and unleashed a powerful force residing within me. I vowed to rise above nature and her self-made balances. That was the moment in time when I truly embraced and released the true potential of the power inside me. What people call darkness, I call power. With my newfound wisdom, I rebelled against the very forces that I had once trusted, and defied nature as I resurrected my only son from the grave.

"Isabella is a descendant of Mordred, and therefore your heir," Ian clarified.

Morgana cackled, "Clever boy." She kept talking as she circled him. "Isabella's amulet is an extension of my power. It was handed down through the generations of my family and grew more powerful with each heir adding power and memories to it. With my extensive experience in dark magic, I was able to tap into the amulet's power across realms, and I retrieved some of the most powerful memories from those who gave power to my amulet."

Ian choked in disbelief and said, "Your revenge knows no

bounds. Merlin's decision was made for the greater good. Life and death are not ours to decide."

She turned to him and spoke, "Corrupted by his ideals, I see. Decisions made for the greater good of whom? It's better to embrace your true nature than to simply accept the world the way it is. It's a pity that you will never experience it. I am the saviour that is necessary to break the Earth Realm free of its confines within nature's rules. I will bring forth a new world where power means supremacy."

Ian, incredulous, responded, "Morgana, what you speak of is madness. I can't imagine what it was like to lose a child, but I know what it is to lose someone you love. It changes you—it even darkens your heart for a time—but that is the nature of life and what it means to truly love someone. What you are talking about is controlling the delicate nature of life, and the balance that now exists."

With a sinister look on her face, she spat, "The Earth Realm is beyond salvation and in need of change. It will be reborn in my image. All that stands in the way of my plan now is you, my darling descendant."

He retorted, "My grandfather loved me unconditionally in a way I don't think I could ever truly understand. He believed in me, and he trusted me to carry on his responsibilities. Above all else, that means ensuring you are never able to break free from your prison."

"Foolish boy," she jeered. "Do you really think you have what it takes to defeat me? We both have formidable strength, and this place cannot hold both of us for long because of our combined power, so one of us will be leaving soon. I have unlimited memories—so much power trapped within the orbs you no doubt saw. So many memories I can tap into to give me unmatched power, and my vast experience makes yours pale in comparison."

He challenged, "There's only one way to find out." He took his grandfather's gold medal out from under his shirt and it began to glow, as did his grandfather's and Merlin's rings.

Morgana smiled and sneered, "Confidence: such a splendid quality. Let's put it to the test, shall we?"

CHAPTER
27

BATTLE OF THE PENDRAGONS

Ian stood face to face with his ancestor, Morgana. She had now put both her hands together and was creating a green, magical ball of energy within her hands. Once completed, she unleashed a strong beam and hurled it at him. In desperation, he put up his hands in defence, and the green beam bounced off him into two directions, like a river hitting a boulder. Still unsure of what he had done, he looked at her, and saw the surprised look on her face at what had transpired. He closed his eyes and could hear his grandfather's voice whispering to him softly, "Trust your instincts, and yours alone." Then he thought to himself, *My lack of experience in manipulating energies around me is my weakness. I need to rely on family heirlooms and memories to battle Morgana—but will that be enough for me to hold my own against her?*

Both rings were now glowing, and he reached and held the gold medal that was around his neck with both of his hands. The combination of the power from the two rings with the power of the medal created a tremendous amount of energy. A beam of bright, white light suddenly unleashed from the medal, but Morgana blocked it with her green magic that again took a circular shape, but the force still knocked her back. She then created twenty mirror images of herself, with her real self hidden among them. They all circled him, each smiling identically.

All the Morganas simultaneously said, "Such strength and power flows through your veins, as it does mine. It's a pity we cannot work together, side by side. You will set me free from this prison, for my time has come to reclaim the Earth Realm and cleanse it of its impurities. For I am Death, and the Destroyer of Worlds, and in being so, I will create a new world. The dawn of a new era is coming, and you are a necessary sacrifice."

At that moment, Ian became frozen, and he began to levitate off the ground as the circle of Morganas created a ring of green energy that bound them together. As all of their eyes were glowing bright green, he remembered his encounter with the Morganian Monks and their Phantoms. Just like the Source Magician, he needed to target the real Morgana quickly and eliminate her clones, as he could feel his life force weakening. He knew her abilities were potent, and that it was going to take a dominant memory to break the spell she was using to trap him. He closed his eyes and remembered a wonderful childhood memory in which he was playing tennis with his grandfather. It was such a heartwarming one and he could see it unfolding in his mind as clear as day. He opened his eyes, which were now glowing white, and discharged the magic within him through the Merlin Ring. It created a powerful white beam of light that destroyed the mirror images one by one in a domino effect until only the original Morgana remained. As soon as she was alone, a white ball of light froze around her, trapping her within it.

Ian could now move again, and he fell back to the ground, as her spell had been broken. He walked over to the trapped Morgana with his eyes still glowing and told her, "You may have your descendants' memories and dark magic, but I have something even stronger: a special, unbreakable bond with a grandfather that always lives in my heart."

She smiled and closed her eyes. When she opened them, they were shining green, and she flung her arms outward, destroying the white force field that had trapped her. He was thrown back, as now it was his spell that had been broken. His eyes were normal again, and she slowly walked toward him. Suddenly, she used her magic to pull him through the air, holding him hovering right in front of her.

She stated, "I know of the bond you had, and continue to hold close to you. I once had that special bond with my brother, but circumstances drove us apart. Uther was special—amazing in his own way—but he lacked the courage to make necessary decisions. Your grandfather was special, as well. Isabella knew this, and she earned his confidence over the years they spent training together. He entrusted her with many things, including some of the memories he shared with you. It was only the power of my amulet that brought forth her dark side and made her strong enough to do what needed to be done, including killing when necessary. This was how she was able to torture your grandfather for his memories about the location of the Merlin Ring and his interactions with Merlin, many of which included how to break me out of this prison."

Ian could talk, but he was still immobile. He recalled the orbs he'd seen containing his memories with his grandfather, and he understood now how they had come to be in Morgana's possession.

He accused, "You are a monster!"

She smiled and said, "You could be right. Monsters inflict fear, and when someone is as feared as I am, they could be perceived as one. As such, no one can resist me and what is coming." Then she leaned forward and whispered in his ear, "Your grandfather was indeed strong, and he was able to block all memories of the sword and Merlin Ring, but he could not block all of them. Eventually, he had to sacrifice some, and the ones he lost were of you. I now possess those—although regrettably, none were as important as I would have liked."

Rage engulfed Ian as he fought to try and free himself.

She spoke softly to him, "You have been defeated, and now you are doomed to spend the rest of your days here." He could feel his life force slipping away from him, second by second, as her dark magic continued to trap and drain him. She was now using his grandfather's memories against him. Even though she did not possess the actual memories, she could still draw powerful magic from them, since she was so experienced in this type of magic.

Ian knew he must trigger his inner magic again, and that meant he needed a very strong memory. He closed his eyes and thought of one of the recent memories he had. It was the moment in the hotel room when he had put the Elite Ring on and was able to talk with his grandfather through the memory of him as a child on Christmas morning. This was an especially meaningful recollection of his, and he used it to trigger the magic within him. His eyes turned white again, and he broke free of her current spell. This time, his magic was so powerful that Morgana was thrown to the edge of the platform/roof. Then the whole tower and roof began to shake, until the upper level of the structure finally broke free from the bottom level and started spinning freely in the grey abyss of the storm that was worsening by the minute. Morgana and Ian were both hanging on to the edge of the upper platform/roof that had broken free. His eyes were bright white, and hers were bright green.

The platform they both managed to climb onto was circling the tower it used to be connected to. It was spinning slowly and rotating end over end, but Morgana was able to defy gravity and walk on it, even when it was upside down. To Ian's surprise, he was able to do the same, and an epic battle of magical powers ensued. Beams of white and green energy were exchanged back and forth. Both were able to block and avoid the incoming bolts of power, but the strain eventually began to take its toll on both of them. Ian was able to match her power, but he knew in order to defeat her and escape this realm, he would need to destroy her. He leapt off the platform to one of the smaller islands circling the tower. His magic gave him incredible strength and agility, and he was able to hop from island to island as they appeared in front of him. Morgana remained where she was, hurling beams at him as she manipulated the platform to follow his path.

He avoided the green energy beams being directed at him, and then he finally lunged for the edge of the lower level of the island he had originally landed on, which was now missing its upper level where Morgana's throne used to be. He pulled himself up and made his way to the orbs of memories.

He stopped partway through the collection of orbs on the main level, noticing memories of him and his grandfather. He knew destroying the orbs would deal a serious blow to her magic and power now that he understood the relevance of the orbs containing memories. He reached out his hand with the Merlin Ring glowing brightly, and a white beam of light emanated from the ring and shot through all of the orbs—but before they could be shattered, Morgana arrived on the island and unleashed a web of green energy, which encircled everything. She ran toward Ian and the orbs. He could feel his power being drained, and his bright white eyes flickered. Her power was too strong, and his magic kept weakening. He fell to his knees as it faded, and he heard her evil, sinister laugh.

There is only one memory that might be powerful enough to stop her, Ian thought, *but it's the most painful one I have.* It was the last memory he had of his grandfather being alive in the Earth Realm. Holding her at bay for the moment with the magic he has conjured, he remembered sitting with his grandfather in the hospital in Montreal. He remembered it like it was yesterday, and his eyes misted.

Inside the memory, Ian slowly got up from his chair in his grandfather's hospital room and laid his head on his grandfather's chest, putting his arms around him. Granddad was in a coma, and this was Ian's last chance to say goodbye. The earthly bond between grandfather and grandson soon extinguished, and this created a pain that never went away.

Only now did Ian understand the true power of that memory; the pain was a result of a loss so deep and profound that he had buried the memory far down within his subconscious. For the first time in many years, he remembered that moment, and a surge of power grew from within him.

"This is for you, Granddad," he cried, "and for the love of our family." He got up from his knees, his eyes glowing strongly again. A blinding white light destroyed the green web of energy, and the orbs shattered into pieces and disintegrated.

Then he made his way over to Morgana. She sat up against one of the pillars, her black garments ripped and tattered, and her head lolling against her chest. She had been reduced to a shell of her former self, and she looked up incredulously as he knelt down beside her on one knee.

She spat, "You may have somehow defeated me, but there are other dark things looming in Earth's and the other realms." With that, her life force began to fade, and she slowly disintegrated into a pile of black ash. Now that the darkness had been vanquished, bright light began to flood the realm.

Suddenly, everything began to shake, and a white vortex of smoke began swirling around Ian. He found himself being pulled back the way he had entered: back through the vortex. He could see the realm around him falling apart. Islands that once floated and circled were now falling, and bright light continued to illuminate the realm he was leaving behind. He closed his eyes, and when he next opened them, he found himself back in the chamber of Excalibur, and his life force had returned to his body. The enchantment stone on Excalibur began to shake and crack, with white light pouring out. It eventually burst into small pieces until it was no more.

He fell to his knees and felt his mother's arms wrap around him. He took a deep breath and hugged her. He said, "It's over, Mom. Morgana is gone. We did it."

"You did it," she corrected. "You saved us all." She helped him to his feet, and to his surprise, Kate came running and jumped into his arms.

Ian asked, "You're okay? When I left, you were in such a weakened state."

"I can't explain it," Kate replied. "I just feel alive with life."

He smiled warmly and responded, "You look beautiful." Then he looked around. "Where is Isabella?"

Lynn spoke up, "You were barely gone a few seconds, but in that short time, she disappeared."

He smiled and said, "It doesn't matter. Morgana has been destroyed, and now Isabella has no one to take orders from. If she returns, I know how to harness my power to combat her darkness."

Lynn queried, "What do we do about the real Excalibur?"

Ian let go of Kate and approached the stone that housed the blade. The Merlin Ring was glowing on his finger, and he felt drawn to the sword. He put his right hand—the one with the ring on it—onto the sword's handle. To his amazement, he was able to pull the sword from the stone. Lynn and Kate looked on in astonishment as he held Excalibur in his hands.

CHAPTER 28

THE BIRTH OF IAN ROBERTS

Ian could feel the power of Excalibur surging through his body. It was a source of incredible power, and as tempted as he was to take the sword for himself, he knew that it must remain here in the chamber where it had been hidden for so long. It belonged with Uther. Still wearing Merlin's and his grandfather's rings and medal, he felt a special power residing within him. He was able to call upon this power to once again plunge the sword back into the stone. As he pulled his hands away, the Pendragon logo appeared on the stone that now housed Excalibur, and then faded away. Excalibur was once again in its rightful place. He knelt down on one knee, placed his hand on Uther's sarcophagus, and offered his thanks, support, and love for his great ancestor's sacrifice of his life for the greater good.

Ian, Kate, and Lynn retraced their steps to exit the chamber. As they made their way up the stairs that had brought them into the Pendragon crypt, Ian was able to use the power of his grandfather's ring to replace Uther's sarcophagus cover behind them. He took one last look at the collection of stone sarcophagi that lay before him before he felt Kate's hand brush against his.

"Come on," she urged, "let's get out of here."

He nodded and took her hand as they climbed the stairs leading outside. Once again, the power of his grandfather's ring was able to open the secret entrance, which allowed them back onto the green fields of Glastonbury, where the sun was just starting to go down. With one final movement of his hand, Ian closed the entrance to the chamber below. As the three walked away, grass reappeared over the entrance, hiding it from the world.

It was late evening in the UK, and they were aboard a flight destined for Montreal. Lynn had the window seat, and as the emotional events of the last few days caught up with her, she fell into a deep sleep. Ian sat in the aisle seat with Kate in the middle, her head on his shoulder. He gently kissed the top of it as she fell asleep. Although exhausted, he was still awake as he thought to himself, *What's next? Do I just return to my normal life? How can I go back to the life I knew?* With these questions floating around in his head, he finally fell asleep.

With the UK being five hours ahead of Montreal, they arrived safely back in Montreal around 9:00 p.m.—approximately the same time they had left. After collecting their luggage, Ian held his backpack with one hand and Kate's with the other while Lynn walked beside him. They exited the airport and caught a taxi to 20 Greene Avenue.

It was dark as they walked through the doors of the house. Ian wandered into the living room, where a collection of pictures hung, showcasing so many moments of his grandparents' life together. He looked closely at a picture of his mother and his Aunt Tessa and smiled. He spoke to his aunt's picture, "We did it, Aunt Tessa, and I will never forget what you did for all of us." He reached into his backpack and took out a small box, which contained both the Merlin Ring and his grandfather's ring. Still smiling, he took out the latter, and put it on.

Instantly, he was back in his Christmas morning memory. His smile grew as, once again, he was face to face with his grandfather, who laughed and said, "Oh my, Grandson. I am so very proud of you. I knew you possessed the courage, strength, and love to succeed me."

Ian was glowing, and he acknowledged, "Granddad, none of what I did, or what I am to become, would even be possible without you. You taught me everything I know. I still have questions—such as, what's next for me? Where do I go from here?"

Reg put his hand on Ian's shoulder and said, "All in good time. You may or may not have figured out by now that both my and Merlin's rings are artifacts that aid you in your times of need. Whether it's to contact us, or to protect you or your loved ones, the rings' properties will always help you out of difficult situations. Now that you have embraced who you are, you should continue to learn Merlin's teachings. There is still much evil in the world, and a lot more about my life that you don't know. This was just the beginning, if you choose to follow in my footsteps."

His image began to fade as Ian cried, "Please, not yet, Granddad!"

"Don't worry," he reassured. "We will have many more opportunities to speak as we are now. You are tired and in need of rest. Your powers have been weakened after the battle with Morgana, and you still have much to learn about how the earth's energies work, and in time, I believe you could be the greatest Merlinian Elite in our history. It's time for the next step—if you are ready?"

Ian nodded. "Yes, I'm ready, and so proud and honoured that you chose me."

As his grandfather disappeared, his voice could still be heard as it tapered off. "No grandfather was as lucky as I was to have such a special grandson. Until next time."

Ian found himself back in the living room, and just as before, not much time had passed. His mother appeared with a cup of coffee. He accepted it gratefully and declared, "We need to do something in memory of Aunt Tessa, Mom. No one will ever know her sacrifice except us, and we need to honour that."

"How about if we plant a tree on this property, and have a plaque made up to attach to it?" she suggested. "It will serve as a constant reminder, and it will last for a very long time."

He smiled his approval, and as he put his arm around her shoulder, his grandfather's ring began to glow once again.

Just then, Kate came into the room. She said, "I think it's time I finally took my place running the firm as my father wanted."

Lynn put her coffee down on a nearby table and put her arms around both Ian and Kate. "I am so proud of both of you. You have grown up so much, and you are now ready and able to carry on your families' legacies."

The ring continued to glow as Ian moved back through the kitchen and onto the porch. Kate, who had followed him there, looked in the driveway and asked, "Where is my car, Ian?"

"We'll pick it up tomorrow. It's still at the tennis club."

The ring glowed a little brighter here, so he headed down the stairs to what was his grandfather's domain at 20 Greene Avenue with Kate and Lynn following. The ring became brighter and brighter as they descended. Once they reached the bottom of the staircase, it became brighter still. They all looked around, wondering what the ring was leading them to.

After a few minutes, Ian cried, "Over here, look!"

Next to the stairs was a wall with a small etching that was also glowing. He continued, "Kate, can you please grab my backpack from upstairs?"

She raced up to get it as he examined the wall. When she returned with it, he opened it and retrieved his grandfather's journal. He flipped to a page he had marked and explained, "It's the symbol of the Merlinian Elite, and it states it can be used as a magical lock, just like the Pendragon symbol locked and hid the chamber of Excalibur." He handed the journal to Kate and placed his hand with the ring over the glowing symbol. It slowly faded, giving way to a small keyhole with the initials "RR" above it. He thought for a moment, and then reached into the backpack and pulled out the set of keys that had been left to him. He flipped through them and found a small one that also had the "RR" initials engraved on it. He put it into the hole and turned gently. He heard a few clicks within the wall and waited.

There was a short rumble as part of the wall slid to the right, revealing an entrance to a hidden room. It was in darkness until he located a light switch just inside the opening, using the glow from the ring to find it. Once lit, a large room stretched out in front of them. Four large drafting tables were filled with piles of documents and books. Shelves held ancient books and scrolls. In the far corner of the room was a massive desk filled with more notebooks, keepsakes, and pictures of family and other people Ian didn't recognize. There were framed parchments on the walls and a huge map of the world.

He had found what the ring had been leading him to. He looked at the large map of the world on the wall, which had detailed notes attached to it. Kate approached and whispered, "This was your grandfather's office. He wanted you to find it and carry on his work. You are now Ian Dekker, Merlinian Elite!"

He grinned and said, "You mean Ian Roberts. It's time I carried my grandfather's good name. As for being an Elite, it's something I have to work towards. As my granddad said to me, this is just the beginning." Ian held Kate close as they looked upon the map of the world. Whatever was to come next, they were ready to face it together.

ACKNOWLEDGMENTS

I would like to sincerely thank and pay tribute to the following individuals who helped shape this book, The Grandfather Chronicles, *The Secret of the Sword*:

- My Mom, for the on-going love, support, and guidance that continue to shape me as a young man.

- My Granny and Granddad (Lillian and Reg Rodricks) – Although you are no longer with us, your memories and impressions made upon me, inspired many of the great moments of this book.

- My Aunt, Pat Rodricks – who helped me shape the ideas from my imagination into a well-told story.

Thank you to the following for their continued support:

- Brian Bell

- Jim Bagozzi

- Brenda Rodricks

- Bernard Poole.

- Ron Laviolette

A very special thanks to:

- Jess Feser – My Publishing Team Lead who always had time to answer my questions with such energy and enthusiasm.

- Hayley Evans – A Professional Editor who worked with me and spent countless hours meticulously critiquing this manuscript to deliver a polished and professional story.

I want to thank EVERYONE who ever took a moment to say something positive to me or took the time to teach me something.

ABOUT THE AUTHOR

Sean Rodricks Bell is a Canadian author. Growing up, his creativity and interests were encouraged by the loving relationship he shared with his grandfather. An avid reader, he has long been fascinated by epic narratives, fantasy literature, Arthurian legends, and powerful villains. Combined, these influences led to the writing of his first book, *The Secret of the Sword*, which is part of his forthcoming series, The Grandfather Chronicles. His imagination and dedication to nurturing family values has helped Sean in creating a world filled with magic that readers of all ages will relate to. He currently resides in St. Catharines, Ontario, with his dog Rocky.